Animal Park

Other Lions titles you may enjoy

Joyce Stranger
Midnight Magic

Caroline Akrill
The Eventing Trilogy
Eventer's Dream
A Hoof in the Door
Ticket to Ride

Patricia Leitch
The Jinny series
1. For Love of a Horse
2. A Devil to Ride
3. The Summer Riders
4. Night of the Red Horse
5. Gallop to the Hills
6. Horse in a Million
7. The Magic Pony
8. Ride Like the Wind
9. Chestnut Gold
10. Jump for the Moon
11. Horse of Fire
12. Running Wild

Animal Sanctuary

②

Animal Park

Joyce Stranger

Lions
An Imprint of HarperCollins*Publishers*

I owe thanks to Ann Cragg and Barbara Emptage of
the Glantraeth Animal Sanctuary, Anglesey,
for letting me share their weekends and "borrow"
their animals for my stories.
To Eileen Clark who rescued the real Blue,
and to Joe Naylor of the Brynterion working farm
for letting me watch a breach calving.
To David, Alison and Mark at the sea zoo
which I have watched grow.
To Les and Denise Edwards whose bitch Jess and
dog Nikos have given me the best pup I ever had.

*The stories in this trilogy are works of fiction; the
events are imaginary; the characters, farms and
villages bear no resemblance to any person or place.*

First published in the U.K. in 1992 in Lions

Lions is an imprint of HarperCollins Children's Books,
a division of HarperCollins Publishers Ltd,
77–85 Fulham Palace Road, Hammersmith,
London W6 8JB

Copyright © 1992 Joyce Stranger-Wilson

The author asserts the moral right to be identified
as the author of the work

Printed and bound in Great Britain by
HarperCollins Book Manufacturing Ltd, Glasgow

Chapter 1

The river was raging after the recent rains. The boy threw the stick for his dog, flinging it high. He held the dog, lest he tried to catch it, and it pierced eye or cheek. The dog pulled and whimpered with excitement, eager to retrieve his trophy. It was a good thick stick that the animal had found for himself, foraging among the trees.

It went too far. The water took it and teased it and tossed it, dragging it into the current, to disappear in midstream. Blue, Martin Slater's German Shepherd, barked in disappointment. Martin, afraid that the dog would plunge into the seething flood, held him by the collar, saying "no" very firmly.

Released, Blue bounded off and searched the margin of the little wood, bringing another stick for his master to throw. It was an endless game and the dog never tired. Martin, at odds with the world, and angry with himself and everyone else, broke the stick into fragments, which he dropped casually at his feet.

The dog, resigning himself to inactivity, flopped down, head on paws, to watch thin sunlight speckle the peaty waves. There were so many days like this. Martin seemed never to have time to play, and the dog missed his long sessions of training.

At least the rain that had fallen all week had eased. Rain meant disaster. Not only flooded fields and danger from the spreading water, but it also meant that the visitors did not come to the Animal Park and that money was tighter than ever.

It was two years since Anna Wyn had started the little sanctuary which was intended to supplement the farm income. But every child who lost interest in a pet brought it to them to look after, and nobody ever provided the money for food. Anna Wyn never said no to any sick or homeless creature, and their needs grew, all the time.

Dilys, her elder sister, was more practical. She worked for a local vet and knew that it was not always possible to save a mortally sick bird, or dog, or cat. The Park had a number of healthy animals, but the little hospital was full of baby birds in need of frequent feeding, of two litters of tiny rabbits, their eyes not yet open, that had been dug out of the ground by a farmer when opening up a drain.

There was also an owl that had been hit by a

train, having decided to hunt along the railway embankment, and a fox cub with a broken leg, found in the road.

Every baby animal meant Anna Wyn spent time feeding, and Martin, the second he reached home from school, was called in to help with the rest of the work.

He tried, as hard as he could, to fit in with his stepfather and stepsisters. He was no longer a rebel, a loner, but did his best to please his mother. It was nearly three years since she re-married. Bitterness caught him, all over again, as he thought of his own father.

He had walked out of their lives when Martin was five years old. He now lived in Australia, with a new wife and young family. He had never had to struggle as Martin's mother had to struggle, keeping herself and her young son by working at the checkout desk in a supermarket until ill health forced her to stay with her sister in Wales.

She had been Gwyn Hughes' housekeeper for a year before she married him. Martin had hated Wales, and hated his new family. Now, he was just settling down but it still didn't seem to work. He refused to take his stepfather's name. He was still Martin Slater. Still his father's son, even if his own father had never wanted him.

Martin's thoughts raced. Even so, he had more than half an eye on the water. There was no way he could leave the sheep to drown. He had escaped, briefly, to think, but thinking didn't seem to get

7

him anywhere. He was looking for peace as there was nothing but turmoil at home. His milling thoughts badgered him and not even the rustle in the trees and the bright eyes of a watching robin could soothe him. His brain seemed to run on the same tracks, re-living the day the anger had begun.

The raging river did nothing to change his mood. It was an added worry and he knew he ought not to be sitting here. Rain in the hills meant the river spilled its banks, and the sheep were isolated, or worse, were thrust into the torrent and drowned. They could wake in the morning to find a lake instead of grass, and a surge of water that carried everything before it. Ducks floated and gulls fished where yesterday the ewes and lambs had grazed.

He should be working now, but, maddened beyond endurance by his stepfather's constant criticism, he had whistled for his dog and escaped, before anyone else was up, to find peace beside the river.

There would be trouble when Martin returned, but so few visitors would come to the Park in this weather that he was not needed. Anna Wyn could cope alone. She made that very clear.

He'd come in search of peace, but there was none here. The rising wind ravaged the trees. There would be a gale tonight. He would have to go back, and tell them the water was over the banks and the sheep in the far meadow must be moved, fast.

He was used to the sudden rush after the rain, and reckoned he had maybe two hours yet before the first creep of the sullen stream to the edge of the field. He needed time to restore his shattered morale, and return able to speak without anger. The day before had brought him to near explosion. Everyone had grumbled at him, even Taid, the girls' grandfather. He was slow. He hadn't groomed the Shetlands. Nobody seemed to realize that he hadn't had time. Whenever he paused for breath somebody asked him to do something else.

He had forgotten to put water in the rabbits' enclosure. He had spilled the water for the pigs, tripping over a length of hosepipe that Anna Wyn had forgotten to clear away.

He wanted to yell at them all, to tell them what he thought of them and their constant demands. He had learned that that would never do. It only made matters worse and labelled him as useless and unco-operative and sulky.

The quarrelling had started at Easter, when the Sanctuary re-opened to the public. They had shut for the winter, at the end of October, but the animals still had to be fed and watered and the cages and enclosures cleaned.

They had all imagined that visitors would flock in, but day after day passed, and very few came. The weather was appalling and on Easter Sunday the bitter winds brought snow, which made life even more difficult.

The arguments rumbled on for most of the summer, breaking out afresh every time a new animal patient was brought in for Anna Wyn to care for.

"I said you could run the Animal Park if it made a profit. I didn't bargain on a hospital where every injured bird or animal in Anglesey was brought to us to heal." His stepfather's voice was angry. That had changed in the past months. Gwyn Hughes was normally a very patient man.

Since that day the topic arose so often that Martin could predict his stepfather's exact words. The worst of all the arguments had occurred the night before.

"This week, you haven't made enough to feed the hamsters, let alone the goats, the pigs, the donkey, the ponies and their foals. And all those birds, and the sick baby rabbits, and the injured owl. You collect creatures as if money came out of a bottomless mine."

Gwyn's voice was raised, his expression furious. He was patient with the animals but all his famly seemed to anger him beyond endurance these days. "The farm's subsidising the Park, and if it weren't for your mother and the farm shop . . . "

Anna Wyn shouted at him. "Leah's not my mother. Martin's not my brother. And if we didn't haven't to keep them too, we'd be a lot better off."

Martin wished he could forget her words. It hurt even to remember. The pain that he thought healed was suddenly acute. He didn't belong anywhere and they hated him. At least his mother had Gwyn. Nobody ever stood up for Martin. If it hadn't been for Taid and Blue he would have run away long ago.

He thumped his fist down on a little rock, bruising his hand, and yelled at the trees. Echoes answered him, pealing from the sky. Blue, unnerved, sat up and stared. Martin grabbed the dog and held him tightly, as if he were a talisman that could ward off misery.

He had been afraid of animals when he came to the farm and most of all afraid of dogs. But that was before a pathetic starving waif crept into his life. Blue was now a magnificent dog with a shining coat. His legs and sides were gold, his saddle black, and his prick ears were an ever changing guide to his mood.

Now, soothed, and comforted, he lay with them flat and watched his master, who was the most important person in his life. "I don't know what I'd do without you," Martin said. The dog's tail beat on the ground.

Martin wondered if his mother were happy. Two stepdaughters and a new husband kept her very busy and at times Martin felt he had been forgotten by everyone. Three years ago there had been just the two of them. And now . . .

There seemed to be furious voices every day. He couldn't get last night's row out of his head. It seemed to go round and round like an old time gramophone record, stuck in a groove.

His stepfather's voice echoed in his mind.

"It's bad enough trying to keep the farm going. Not one more animal. I mean it. I don't care if it's sick, or dying, or destitute. We have more than enough."

Anna Wyn's animals were more important to her than anything else in her life.

"What am I supposed to do? Let them all die?" She raged out of the room.

The bang of the door was succeeded by an uneasy silence.

Taid, the girls' grandfather, stood up wearily, and limped across the kitchen.

"I'll be off," he said, hating arguments. He flicked his fingers to his dogs, and they went out with him, seeking peace in his cottage across the yard. "Taid's showing his age," Gwyn said. "Don't know what I'll do when he can't help at all."

That was another worry. Taid was the only friend that Martin had. The old man understood how he felt. In the three years since his mother's re-marriage, Martin and Taid, his stepsisters' grandfather, had become very close. One day Taid wouldn't be there at all. He was looking very frail and sometimes found it too much effort to get out of bed.

The water was spilling over the bank. Martin stared at it, yet seemed unable to move. He didn't want to go home. He didn't have a home. Just a place to live. He wanted an end to arguments. He wanted to be part of a real family.

When he let himself out of the house early that morning, he was intending to seek consolation with his friends, the Pritchards, an American family who were on a protracted visit to Wales, to search out their ancestors. They had fallen in love with the country and were writing up its legends. Two books had already been published and they were working on a third.

Martin often wished that Tom Pritchard were his father.

The Pritchards never quarrelled the way his family did. He walked Blue for several miles, and then, at ten o' clock, knowing he ought to be back on the farm, turned down the lane that led to their home. When he reached the huge caravan, he was aware of an uneasy atmosphere.

Martin was longing to talk to Tom, as he had a new idea for a crowd pulling attraction at the Animal Park. The big American always listened.

Today something was wrong with them too. Midge mocked, Tag was sullen, and in the end Martin only said that he had thought of another way of making the farm pay.

Nobody listened. Tom Pritchard was abstracted. His wife was racing to reach the hairdresser for an early appointment. Tag, who Martin had rescued when a wall fell on him two years before, went out to ride his pony. He had plagued his father to buy the little animal, but now he was growing bored. Tag, so named because he had tagged after everyone when he was little, was often off on his own now that he was older. Martin couldn't even remember the child's real name.

Riding the pony was preferable to staying indoors with his family, and Tag had no time for Martin. Midge, his sister, teased him and mocked both boys.

"Sorry, Martin," Tom said. "I've an article to finish and get in the post today."

They had let him down too.

Martin, even more irritated than he had been at the start of the visit, had left then.

The water was still rising. The little tump of grass some yards in front of him was no longer visible. He felt no urgency. He felt as if nothing mattered any more. Nobody would care if he fell into the water and drowned.

The sheep would drown.

He sat and argued with himself. If he ran all the way home it would only take twenty minutes. Plenty of time for Gwyn to shift them. Anyway, what did he owe Gwyn? What did he owe any of them? Let the beastly animals drown. But he knew he couldn't do that. He leashed the dog, lest he jumped into the flooding stream. The current was fierce.

Martin pulled his note book out of his pocket. There must be something they could do to improve matters on the farm. It had to be a success. If not, maybe Gwyn would send Martin and his mother away and they would be as poor as they had been before the marriage. Martin was only

14

just beginning to realize that he and his mother needed their new family much more than the family needed them.

It would be years before he could earn enough to keep them both. He resented being so young, and longed for the time to pass. If only he were eighteen. That was centuries away.

He looked at the figures. No matter how he added them, they still spent far more on animal food than the Sanctuary earned from visitors. Martin had suggested they kept a day-by-day record, thinking it would help, but it hadn't. It made matters worse as the summer was wet and few people wanted to visit an outdoor attraction. All that anyone saw was defeat.

Two farms in the district had sold up, unable to survive. Another farm, that started an Animal Trail, had given up too, in despair. Shops were closing in Bangor and Beaumaris. Friends were out of work, or made redundant.

Their farm went struggling on, trying to balance books that seemed never to balance at all. And unless they had more good barns, there was no way they could put all the animals under cover, and avoid the hazards of rainy days.

"If pigs could fly . . . " Taid said, whenever Martin produced yet another idea. The trouble was that all his ideas cost money they didn't have.

But he had a good idea now. He knew it was a winner, and he longed to share it, but nobody would listen. He knew that he would have to argue. Unless he could produce his plan at such a developed stage that it impossible to dismiss.

If only he could persuade Mervyn Plas Towyn to let him have what he wanted at a price he could afford. If only he could think of some way of earning more money, and helping Anna Wyn with the invalids.

He'd call at Plas Towyn on his way home. The old man had just what he needed and seemed to have no use for it. Martin would have to overcome shyness to do so. He had never spoken to the neighbouring farmer, who discouraged visitors and had a reputation for bad temper.

He looked again at the water. It was crawling towards him. He saw that the grass only a few feet in front of him was already covered. The river was rising faster than it ever had before. There had been so much rain. He shouldn't have stayed so long.

He whistled to Blue. There were over eighty sheep in the river field, and when it boiled over the banks, it carried stock away with it. He had a vision of dead sheep floating, and his stepfather blaming Martin for not telling them in time. Panic spurred his flying feet down the hill. No time to call on Plas Towyn now.

Dog and boy raced headlong, leaping patches of heather, crashing through the growing bracken, Blue catching his master's mood. The dog knew that they had to hurry, though he did not know why.

An hour and a half, maybe. They could still herd the sheep when they were ankle deep in water. If only the banks didn't burst. If only he had realized . . . if only he hadn't been day dreaming.

Please, God, let me be in time.

He could never let any animals die needlessly.

The ground was uneven and he had to slow, panting, afraid lest he fell and broke an ankle. The sheep would never be saved then.

Although he was gasping for breath and had a stitch in his side, he pelted on.

Chapter 2

Martin pelted down the track that led to the road to Bryn Gwynt. He was worried about the sheep, worried he'd waited too long. Even so, his mind was full of his plan for the Park.

He'd been nursing the idea of the Noah's Ark for weeks. He had a vision of it, restored and painted in bright colours, the ark building on top, an enormous Wendy house filled with carved animals, bright little stools that Taid would make and paint, and miniature tables. If only Mervyn would let him have the boat at a price he could afford.

The old boat was almost derelict. Once it had been a heavy fishing boat, meant for day trips. Now it was rotting and forgotten. He had often seen it as he passed Mervyn Plas Towyn's farm.

Martin had discovered he had a talent for woodwork. He was always top of the class. There was satisfaction in taking a piece of plank, in planing and smoothing and shaping it. There was satisfaction in the finished product, too, the wood shining under his vigorous polishing. He could polish away anger and frustration and fury, and go home soothed and refreshed.

There would be even more satisfaction when he took his masterpiece home and saw their astonishment.

He was eager now, anxious to bargain with Mervyn for the boat. He would surely not want it, an old thing like that, lying out in all weathers, rotting away.

He had never visited the farm. "Terrible there since his wife died," Jones the Milk said. "Going to ruin, and the old man with heart trouble too. Ought to give up. And above all, ought not to have that bull. Old devil, that bull."

That bull had been a source of worry to the village for some time. Martin in the past two years had changed his mind about most animals, but he was terrified of Hero, the Plas Towyn bull, and always passed the farm warily on his way home from the school bus stop.

The farm gates were falling apart and twice Hero had escaped onto the road. So far, he had done no harm, but he was immense and Mervyn was old, and losing his strength.

The moorland ended as the farm walls appeared.

19

Blue ran through the shallows of the little brook, splashing, his eyes alight with fun. Martin, crossing by the stepping stones, had just reached the other side, which was within a stonechuck of the Plas Towyn farm, when he heard a terrified yell.

Two figures he thought he recognized from school slipped out of the farmyard, over the wall, and raced off down the road. That meant trouble. It always did when those two were around.

The bull was out in the yard.

Martin stared at him, his throat suddenly dry. The beast was even larger than he had thought. His great horns spread outwards from his head as he charged.

Martin raced along the wall towards the five-barred gate. Mervyn was spreadeagled against the wall, unable to move, pinned in the corner of the yard.

Something had to be done and done fast. There was only Blue to do it.

Martin's voice was urgent.

"Blue, over." His dog was at risk, but he couldn't sacrifice the man when there was a chance of deflecting the bull. With Mervyn penned against the wall, there could only be one outcome.

As the dog leaped into the yard, the bull turned and lumbered towards him. Martin vaulted over, and flew to the shed where Mervyn's two sheepdogs were barking at the tops of their voices, aware that something was wrong. Three dogs were better than one.

The dogs slammed against him as he opened the door. He picked himself off the ground. They needed no commands. They had heard their master's fear. They raced towards Hero, as he turned again towards the old man.

Blue was at Hero's head, barking. The two dogs at his sides barked and snapped. Bewildered, the animal put down his head and charged the smaller sheepdog. She leaped at his shoulder, bit, and was off again, over the cobbles, ready to race in for another attack.

Martin put an arm round the old man, propelling him to the gate, pushing him through, slamming the gate behind them. His fear seemed to lend him strength. He and Mervyn stood side by side, watching the dogs, helpless, sure that one or all of them would die before the now maniac charges.

Neither of them noticed the car that drew up in front of the house. Its driver leaped out and ran towards them.

"Dear God," he said. Martin recognized Dai the sheep, who had once been a fireman, and was now retired. "Your gun, man. Or we'll all be dead."

Mervyn, blue-lipped and white-faced, pointed to the kitchen. It seemed an age before Dai reappeared, the loaded gun in his hands. The dogs were tiring. The bull lowered his head again. Twm, the younger sheepdog, exhausted and unable to dodge, slid through the bars of the gate and dropped panting at his master's feet. The gate shuddered as the bull charged at him, but it withstood the impact. This time.

Mervyn seemed unable to move, although Martin was desperate to remove him from danger. Neither Martin or Dai could call off the other two dogs. They were intent on challenge. Blue's great bark sounded as the bull charged the older sheepdog. Mog leaped the wall and stood on his hind paws, barking. Twm, restored by his rest, wise with experience and used to sheep that sometimes rebelled against him, ducked in, aware that he was dealing with something far more dangerous than any ram.

As the sharp teeth sank into the powerful hind leg Hero turned again, kicking out at the dog, who ducked aside.

Blue raced at the furious beast. The bull faced him. The dog ran across the yard, now showing weariness.

Hero pounded towards the gate, hooves thunderous on the cobbles. Mog ran in and nipped again. The bull stopped, his lowered head swaying, both hind legs bleeding.

"Need your dog out of the way," Dai said. "Can't risk a shot yet."

The bull shook his head, and lowered it, ready to attack again. Blue was tiring.

Martin whistled. This time his dog fled across the cobbles and joined him at the gate, where he lay, panting. The collie lay flat, as if herding sheep. Martin wondered at the courage of the dog.

The gun cracked.

For a moment Martin thought that Dai had missed his target. The great head lowered, and then the bull fell, shot through the eye.

Mog crept to his master, behaving as though he thought he was responsible for the death and deserving of a thrashing.

Mervyn slumped suddenly to the ground, his face wet with sweat. "Got me against the wall. Distracted when you came, boy. Good job you were there. He'd have killed me, else."

"You'd better come to our house," Martin said. "Can you walk to Dai's car?"

"Not my legs that's hurt. It's my chest, boy. Can't get my breath. He didn't touch me."

"Saw the village bad lads running off," Dai said. "Did they let him out?"

Mervyn nodded.

"Owed me a grudge." It was difficult to talk. "Came for trick or treat last Hallowe'en. No treat. I've no time for nonsense." He managed to stand, clinging on to Dai, trying to breathe more easily. "They let all the cattle on to the road for their trick. One calf killed by a car. Took two days to get them all back again. I had the police on them. They've never forgiven me. Up to mischief here whenever they can. War, it is."

"Drive you, now," Dai said. "Martin's Mum'll give you a meal and a rest. Get in. Gwyn'll help out; always willing."

It seemed a century before they arrived at

Bryn Gwynt. Martin was aware of the old man's painful breathing. When they reached the cobbled yard, Blue went to his place outside his daytime kennel.

Cariad, once a pet lamb, now old and doddery, stumbled over to inspect the newcomer.

"Martin," his mother said, as he opened the door. "How often have I asked you . . . " She stopped.

"Mervyn's bull attacked him," Martin said.

His stepfather was on his feet at once, helping the farmer to a chair, while Anna Wyn, Martin's younger stepsister, flew to the phone.

"Doctor or ambulance?" she asked.

"Doctor," Mervyn lay back, his face taut with pain. "Can't afford time in hospital . . . nobody to help."

"We'll help." Gwyn looked over at Martin. "All of us."

Dai had come into the room. He rubbed his hand through his thick wiry grey hair. "Goes for me too," he said.

Martin knew what a disaster it was when the only man on the farm was laid up. Plas Towyn, like their farm, was a family effort, and there was only Mervyn since his wife died.

For the time being, Martin had forgotten all about the boat.

Chapter 3

"Two lambs were swept away," Anna Wyn said, her eyes accusing Martin.

"Did you get the rest in safely?" Leah's face was anxious.

"Yes. No thanks to Martin. He ought to have come home and told us as soon as he saw the water rising." Gwyn was angry. He hated losing stock.

"I'd have been here sooner if it hadn't been for the bull." It wasn't fair. If he hadn't dallied, Mervyn might be dead. The old man lay back in the chair, his face still grey.

"Tag rode by, and came in to see us. He told us you went to the river bank at around ten o'clock. It's now after twelve. Saturday's one of our busiest days and you haven't cleaned the stables."

Thank you, Tag, Martin thought. Who was

going to visit them when the rain was pouring down in sheets, he wondered, but said nothing. It was no use. He hated all of them. He thought that they had accepted him and they hadn't. Everything he did was wrong, even when he tried his hardest. If he hadn't gone out at all, who would have saved Mervyn? Blue had held the bull off while Martin got the old man out of the target area.

"If I'd come home earlier I wouldn't have seen the bull," he said. "What did you do? Dai and the dogs did everything necessary," Anna Wyn said. Dai hadn't seen Martin drag Mervyn out of range. he hadn't been there at the start. "All you did was stand and stare and lose us two lambs."

Martin wanted to hit his stepsister. He had been terrified out of his wits when he went into the yard with the rampaging animal charging at them. He looked at the old farmer, but he was still too exhausted to talk. He lay back with his eyes closed.

"Never known the water come up so fast," Taid said. "Drink your coffee, boy. Warm you."

"He ought not to have been out at all. We need all the help we can get and he goes skiving."

Martin picked up his cup. Blue shot across the farmyard to the gate and barked.

"Must be the doctor," Gwyn said.

Nobody came.

"Scared of the dog." Dai went outside and then ran to the gate. Blue was barking frantically at a dilapidated cardboard box that had been left just outside.

Dai picked the box up and carried it into the kitchen. Blue followed him, his eyes eager, his tail waving slowly, as if unsure of himself.

Anna Wyn opened the box.

Her yell startled all of them.

"I hate people." Inside, crouched down, staring at her with anguished eyes, were two small cats, one ginger, one black and white. She lifted out the black and white, although he tried desperately to cling to his dismal sanctuary.

He mewed pitifully.

Dai had left the door open. The ginger cat sprang out of the box, bolted across the kitchen, and out into the yard. She was heavily pregnant.

Blue raced after her. Martin yelled.

"Blue, down."

The dog dropped on the cobbles. The ginger cat vanished into the barn. The black and white cat, seizing his opportunity, scratched Anna Wyn's hand, snatched the half biscuit she was holding, and jumped on to the highest dresser shelf, where he crouched, his green eyes glowering.

Gwyn called to Blue, who came into the kitchen, his head hanging, his tail between his legs, aware he had done wrong, but not quite sure how.

The black and white cat spat at him.

"Lie down, Blue," Martin said. He looked anxiously at Mervyn, who was lying back in his chair. The old man's colour was better.

"Cat's injured," the old man said.

There was a gaping cut on the little animal's

shoulder, matted with fur that was clotted with blood. Martin suddenly found himself echoing his stepsister's anger. That was a knife wound. It couldn't be anything else.

"Can't do a thing about that yet," Anna Wyn said. "He's terrified. It'll be days before he lets us touch him. Have to get Dilys to bring anti-biotics to put in his food. I hope he won't die."

"Doesn't look anywhere near death to me," Taid said. "Full of life, that one is, and fighting us as well as his injuries."

Leah, Martin's mother, poured milk into a saucer and set it on the shelf. The cat stared at her, his eyes astonished, and then began to lap so greedily that they knew he was famished.

Blue's bark alerted them yet again as the doctor drove into the yard.

Martin went out to the stables. Better get them cleaned, or there would be more trouble. He did not hear Taid come up behind him.

"Don't worry too much," the old man said. "Gwyn can't get at God or the Government so he takes it out on us. All of us, not only you. What happened at Plas Towyn today?"

He picked up a pitchfork and worked alongside Martin, who told him about the way the dogs had held the bull off and he had managed to drag the old man outside.

"He would have been killed if I hadn't come then," Martin said. The old man sighed.

"Aye. You did a good job. But we never get

credit for what we do right; only blame for what we do wrong."

That didn't make Martin feel much better. Taid was the only one who ever comforted him though he had an odd way of doing it. Blue stayed in the yard, lying by the back door, on guard.

"Martin," his mother said, appearing at the stable door as they raked the last of the soiled straw into the barrow. "Would you mind if Mervyn has your room, and you sleep in Taid's spare room for the next week or so? The doctor doesn't think he needs to go to hospital. He does need looking after, though. The doctor said he was to spend at least a week in bed."

Martin wasn't too sure about somebody else sleeping in his room. It was his sanctuary. But he had no choice. Good might come of it. Maybe Mervyn would give him what he wanted out of gratitude. Nobody knew of his brainwave yet.

"Lunch is ready." His mother went indoors. Martin emptied the barrow and followed Taid. They shed their wellingtons in the porch and padded over the cold tiles, to scrub in the scullery sink.

The black and white cat had retreated again to the back of the shelf. His fur was no longer fluffed and he had stopped swearing at them. The matted wound looked worse now that the cat was resting, but any move towards him resulted in a spitting fury.

"We need to find the ginger cat and feed her and

make sure she isn't injured too," Anna Wyn said. "The last thing we want is for her to have kittens in the barn. They'll be as fierce as wildcats and very difficult to catch and find owners for."

Night came and the ginger cat still remained hidden. Leah put a saucer of food on the barn floor, and hoped that she would eat.

Martin, passing the building on his way to Taid's cottage, heard a rustle in the straw and peeped in. The moon shone on the little cat, crouched, concentrating on her food. He stood still, afraid that if she smelled him or heard him she might retreat.

She was in a strange place and frightened, and felt as alien as he did. He hoped she could sense his sympathy. They were both outcasts, given unwilling shelter. He was no better off than any of the strays, but nobody offered him much comfort.

His misery made his throat ache.

The wind, blowing away from the barn, gave the cat no warning of his presence. When she had eaten she washed herself diligently and then vanished in the straw. She was going to be very difficult to catch.

Next day was Sunday.

"Operation Plas Towyn," Gwyn said, as soon as they had eaten breakfast, hours after the early morning chores had begun. He and Dai had driven to the other farm the night before to feed the animals and milk the cows.

Leah put out food for the black and white cat, who still refused to come down from his shelf while there were people in the room. But he had used the litter tray that had been put down for him the night before, so at least he was house-clean.

Mervyn stayed in bed. He protested, unused to inactivity, but Leah was firm. Martin's bed was by the window, looking out over the cobbled yard. Blue waited by the back door, hoping that he too would be part of the day's activities.

Martin took up the breakfast tray.

"Never been spoiled like this in my life," the old man said. "Lucky you came by yesterday. The bull would have killed me. You did bravely, boy."

Martin felt a small glow of pleasure. Nobody else had praised him, except maybe Taid in his quirky fashion. He liked the old man and felt as if he had a stake in keeping him alive.

"He didn't touch you?"

"No. I managed to dodge. Too old for running. That was what did for me. He'd been teased before they let him out. Poking him with sticks. I yelled at them, but they took no notice. Ran fast enough when he came out. I think he charged the door, and surprised them. Best bull I ever had. But Dai had no choice."

He sighed heavily.

"I was coming to see you," Martin said. "Only I saw the river rising and was racing home. I'd have called in again, though. I wondered if you'd sell me that old boat by your house?"

31

"That old thing? Never sail again. Not fit for anything but burning, Bach. What would you want with it now?"

"I want to make a Noah's Ark for the childrens' playground," Martin said. "It would be fun for the kids, and fun to do, too. Nobody else has an Ark."

The old man looked at him thoughtfully.

"Too rotten. There's another boat in the barn; smaller, but solid. I owe you, Bach. You can take that and welcome. Only one thing though."

Martin looked at him, wondering what condition was to be set.

"You let me help with ideas. Used to do a lot of woodwork in my time. Have to sell up Plas Towyn. Useless to pretend I can manage. I can't. Maybe I can help out here. Still do as much as Elwyn." It was a moment before Martin realized that Elwyn was Taid's christian name. Nobody ever used it.

The farmer began to eat his boiled egg. "Ask your Da to look at Lola. She's due to farrow any day now; she needs watching or she lies on her piglets. A prolific mother, but a daft animal."

"Martin!" his stepfather called up the stairs.

Martin grinned at Mervyn and left the room.

By the time they reached Plas Towyn the knacker had removed the carcase of the bull.

Mervyn's two dogs greeted them vociferously, as they split up to get to work.

Leah and Anna Wyn busied themselves with spring cleaning. Dai, who had driven over in his own car, went in to milk the cows.

Martin, feeding and cleaning out chickens and ducks and geese, remembered the sow. As soon as he had collected the eggs, he went to look for her. The outbuildings contained calves and chickens and ducks. The Large White sow was in the last sty that he opened.

He had never seen any pig so mountainous. She stared at him from tiny eyes and grunted.

"We'll have to take her home. Can't keep twenty-four-hour watch over her. Too much to do at Bryn Gwynt. I'll go for the trailer," Gwyn said from behind him. "Hope she doesn't produce any piglets before we get her back."

He vanished.

Martin explored the barns and the remaining outhouses. In the furthest building he found the boat. It was small, sturdy and clinker built. Very solid. He'd need a hoist to get it on to the back of a lorry; maybe Dai knew someone who could help transport it.

There was room for a very large Wendy house on top; he visualized it, brightly painted, and felt his fingers itching to begin work. He was still daydreaming when Gwyn returned.

"For heavens' sake, boy. Stop mooning. You should have gone to help your mother if you can't find anything else to do. There's a power of work to get through. Now lay a trail of pig nuts from Lola's sty to the trailer ramp."

That's right. Grumble, Martin thought. His hands were sore from all the work he'd done that morning. He'd cleaned out sty after sty. Mervyn seemed to have neglected his animals for some days. He'd avoided the bull pen. That brought frightening memories. It stood there, empty, but haunted.

Lola, unlike the Vietnamese pot-bellied sow that Anna Wyn had bought two years before, knew all about trailers. They always took her to the boar. This was her sixth litter, so that in her mind they were linked with pleasure. She ambled along, eating as she went, marched up the ramp and settled her vast body on the straw.

"Animals," Gwyn said. "They never do what you expect. Thought we'd have trouble. Better feed her, boy. She'll be ravenous with that lot inside her. Twelve at least, I'd reckon."

By lunchtime the farmhouse shone with polish, the farmyard was swept and clean and all the animals fed. The two dogs, forlorn, went into their shed.

Gwyn looked at them.

"Better keep Blue indoors, and give them his daytime pen for their own," he said. "Can't leave them shut up all day, and all night too. They were out by day with Mervyn and in the farmhouse in the evening. Only sleep in the shed at night."

The excited collies leaped into the back of the Land Rover and sat either side of Martin, looking out of the windows, barking at anything that moved. They were noisy companions.

"Not used to travelling. Mervyn never takes his

dogs around," Gwyn said, negotiating the turn into the lane that led home. The hawthorn hedges were spangled with wild briar roses, the lane edge bright with summer flowers half- hidden in the grass.

"Sunday lunch'll have to be sandwiches," Leah said, moving painfully. "It's hard working on a house that hasn't been properly cleaned for months."

As they climbed out of the Land Rover, Blue ran to greet them, followed by Gwyn's two sheepdogs. Mervyn's two collies piled out of the van, and flew at the other dogs, barking and snapping.

Within seconds the yard was noisy with snarl and snap of the fight.

Martin jumped out fast, not knowing what to do, but sure that something must be done, and quickly, or all three would be injured. Taid, who had erupted from his cottage, held Martin's arm.

"Can't interfere, boy. If we do, we'll get bitten. Should have tied Mervyn's dogs inside the Land Rover. They accepted Blue as an ally yesterday, with the bull to tackle, but it's a different story now. My two don't know them. Trespassers, they are, to our dogs. Our fault . . . too late now. Lucky mine were shut in, or we'd have five at it."

Martin watched the rolling huddle. First Blue, then a collie was on top. The fight swayed to and fro across the cobbles. Blue was underneath, with the four collies snarling above him. He shook himself free, and flew in again, furious.

None of them saw Mervyn appear in the kitchen

35

doorway, wearing a borrowed dressing gown. He walked across the yard.

Martin, appalled, expected to see blood spurt from any one of the dogs, or to see Blue fall under what appeared to be a mass attack. Behind him a cat yowled and the geese and ducks and hens began to cackle.

What on earth could they do?

None of them saw Mervyn connect the hose to the tap and turn the water on. They were startled by the sudden hiss of water. He directed the nozzle at the dogs, soaking them. The group of snarling animals split up, each creeping away dejectedly, aware of having sinned. Blue shook himself.

"Porch," Martin said, his voice fierce. The dog was too wet to go indoors. Gwyn called his two collies, and kennelled them.

"Yours can go in Blue's compound," he said, turning to the old man, who was holding both his struggling animals. "I thought it better to have them here than on their own. Too much to-ing and fro-ing to feed and exercise them."

Martin dried his dog and examined him carefully for bites. Blue was limping on his left foreleg. He had probably strained it. Martin sighed. Life was never easy. Next day was school and he would have to rely on the family to keep the German Shepherd out of trouble. The two extra dogs were certainly going to cause problems.

Chapter 4

Monday dawned, and school started. There was no way of escape. A fine day, a blue sky with high clouds, and a wind that promised to roar later but now was only a whisper among the trees. Martin looked up at the hills and wished that he and Blue were alone, climbing, away from the world. No one to criticise or condemn.

He wished the journey to school were longer. He needed much more time to think. There were so many things they could do to improve the Animal Park and attract more visitors. There never was any time at all at home. He was busy helping round the farm as soon as his homework was done, and dropped into bed exhausted. His day began at 6 a.m., when he collected eggs and cleaned out the chickens, before walking Blue.

He was tired before the day began. Today he was angry, too, as the morning had begun badly. He tripped and fell while carrying a basket of eggs. More than half had broken.

"Why we have to put up with a stupid lump like you, heaven only knows," Anna Wyn said, rescuing those that were unharmed.

"Can't you do anything right, boy?" his step-father asked, exasperated, as Martin tried to clear up the broken shells from the ground and the cats had a feast of eggyolk. "Get off to school and leave us in peace. Take more care, next time."

"I'll do the eggs. He can't be trusted to do anything properly." Anna Wyn's voice was as angry as her eyes. Martin had a lump in his throat and a longing to get away, anywhere. Even to school. He tried so hard to make the Sanctuary a sucess, but everything he thought of was mocked, and everything he did seemed to go wrong. This last idea was a winner, and it couldn't possibly fail.

The bus turned in at the school gates, and there was no time to develop his plans further. But they niggled at the back oif his mind all day.

He came home, new ideas burgeoning. He longed to talk but everyone was rushing around. Someone had opened the top gate and there were over fifty ewes and lambs on the road, being herded up and down by cars.

"At least no-one can blame me," Martin thought, as he walked into the kitchen. "I wasn't even here."

Gwyn put his two dogs into the Land Rover.

"We'll be losing the sheep," Martin's mother said. "As if there wasn't enough bad luck. It's one of the worst years we've ever had." She pushed her hair out of her eyes. "Not even time to get to the hairdresser. Martin, there's a tray for Mervyn on the kitchen table. Can you take it up to him, and have a word or two with him? The poor old fellow's been alone all day." She disappeared through the door.

The tray was covered by a white cloth. Martin removed it, and checked. Cold meat and chicken, green salad and potato salad. No salt or pepper. He put them beside the plate, whistled to Blue, and went off upstairs.

Mervyn was propped up in bed, his colour better than the day before.

"Saw them and shouted," he said. "Didn't do any good. The gate was open and the sheep out before you could say blue moon. Had a dog to herd them out, and then on to the road. It was all planned."

Martin put the tray down on the bed.

"Did you see their faces?"

"Wore caps and scarves. Blue jeans and jacket. Might be anyone." he sighed. "That's a good dog you've got, boy. Brave too. He tackled the bull like a veteran."

He began cutting into the chicken slices.

"Time to talk, boy?"

Martin perched himself on the window seat. "Will you go back to the farm?" he asked.

"Been thinking. Never had time to think before. All day, here. Not sensible, is it? I'll be eighty next year. Sell up . . . I'll need the money to live on. No pension for farmers, and the state don't give that much."

Martin was looking out over the Park, beyond which the fields sloped upwards to the little rocky peak.

"Where would you live?" he asked.

"The old cottage. If I get enough for the farm, I can do it up. Don't want to go away from my old haunts. Maybe could do a bit here, till my heart betrays me."

"Like what?" Martin asked, wondering how on earth any man of that age could be of use.

"Can still feed a baby bird with mealworms," Mervyn said. "Don't need much strength for that. Just a knack and time. Free Anna Wyn for other jobs."

"We brought your sow over. She hasn't farrowed yet," Martin said.

"She'll start about six o' clock tomorrow morning."

Martin stared at him.

"I can predict that to an hour. You ask your Da. Often called me in to tell him when a cow would calve. It annoys the vets." Mervyn chuckled, and his eyes suddenly sparked with mischief. "Those young men can't do it."

Through the window, Martin watched as the sheep spilled through the yard, the dogs behind them. When they were all safely into the field, his mother shut the gate. The Land Rover rocketed into the yard behind her and stopped with a scream of tyres. "Pointless and stupid," Mervyn said, as Gwyn climbed down and whistled to the dogs.

"That old boat." The old man turned his attention to a bowl of fruit salad and cream. "Not much of a way to say thanks for saving my life. Give you Lola and her litter. Any money you make can go into the sanctuary; maybe keep a sow or two and breed from them. She's good for several litters yet and she always has fourteen or more. You could start your own herd . . ."

He leaned back on the pillows. "Off you go, boy. Talking's tired me."

Martin took the tray, signalled to Blue, and went out, looking back before he shut the door. Mervyn's eyes were closed and he looked every year of his age.

Lola and her babies. How much would the little pigs fetch when sold? And how much would be profit? How long would he keep them? And did they have room?

He didn't hear the tentative knock at the door. Blue barked. Martin, about to rebuke him, saw him standing by the back door, his head on one side, expectant. Someone was there that he knew.

He opened the door, and Tag rushed in. Blue met him with waving tail, sniffing diligently at his knees in their blue jeans.

"That stupid pony broke my arm," Tag wailed. His right arm was plastered and held in a sling. "I don't want him. You can have him. He's a horrible animal."

"Hang on," Martin said. "We can't afford him."

"Dad says he'll pay you livery keep for him."

Martin knew the pony would be an asset. They could give rides every day instead of just at weekends.

"Tell your dad we'll take Caley. The end of the barn has a stall in it, and there used to be a horse there. GIve us a week or two."

He ought to ask Gwyn. He ought not to make decisions on his own.

There was a soft mew at his feet. He looked down. Anna Wyn, coming into the kitchen, looked too. The ginger cat had come inside and was asking for food.

"Oh no," she said. "She's had her kittens. In the barn. Now we'll not find them till they're about six weeks old and they'll be hard to tame."

Blue nosed the visitor. She slapped him angrily with her paw. Four bright scratches sprang red across his nose. He retreated to the corner of the room and lay still, his head on his paws, his eyes forlorn. The sharp claws hurt.

The ginger cat mewed again. Nursing mothers needed food and the only way to get it was to ask the humans. She rubbed against Tag's legs.

Anna Wyn opened a tin for her. They all watched when she began to eat as if she hadn't ever been fed in her life before. As she ate, she purred, long and loud and low.

Chapter 5

The days were impossibly busy, but somehow they managed and even had a very little time to spare. Then, in the first week of July, Martin was sent home from school with a tummy infection that refused to clear up for well over a week.

By the time he had recovered, Gwyn, who was never ill, was in bed with a high temperature, Leah was feeling rotten, and dared not go outside, and Anna Wyn was so busy that she had no choice but to keep Martin home from school for several days to help.

Convalescent, she said.

He wearied fast on his first day back at work. He felt as if he had been ill for weeks, but there was no time to think about that. Someone had to care for all the animals.

Every water container in the aviary had to be taken out, washed and re-filled. Floors had to be swept, and after that there was food to take to every creature, and the bowls and buckets to wash out. Martin's legs ached as the food store was at the far end of the field, and many of the enclosures were several hundred yards away from it.

Maggie, one of the Shetlands, kicked her bucket over. Then, irritable because her routine had been interrupted and she had not yet been fed, she stamped on Martin's foot.

By the time they had finished he was aching all over. He longed to go back to bed. No chance of that at all. Wearily, he stumbled indoors, wondering if his back had actually broken or only felt as if it had. He wondered how Anna Wyn managd to lug the straw bales and the sacks of food. They all seemed to weigh a ton.

Leah had baked Cornish pasties, although she herself was surviving on air eked out with egg custard and aspirins. Gwyn had no desire to eat. Mervyn, now much better, was staying with Taid. Both old men had been told to keep well away.

Martin took a pasty from the oven and dropped into a chair. He had never worked so hard in his life. He was almost too tired to eat.

Blue put his head on his master's knee, asking forgiveness, though he was not sure why. He had been banished all day to one of the outhouses. The dog was sure this was a punishment for some unidentified crime. Leah couldn't do with him in the kitchen and the German Shepherd was better shut away, as Mervyn's dogs barked at him every time he passed their compound, and the noise drove everyone crazy.

Gwyn, his head aching, his temper foul, yelled for peace.

Dilys, as yet untouched by the bug that hit all of them, was late home. She came into the kitchen just as Gwyn crawled down the stairs in his dressing gown, and dropped into his arm chair.

Dilys, helping herself lavishly to pickles, sat on the window seat.

"Tag brought the pony over just as I came in," she said. "Nice little Welsh Mountain. It'll be better here all the time, and not just at weekends. Anna Wyn can give rides during the week. I put him in the end stall in the barn. He'll need feeding. I gave him a haynet. I told Tag to go home, in case he caught our bug too."

Caley. Martin was appalled. He had forgotten he had told Tag to bring the pony over. It had seemed a good idea at the time. The livery money would pay easily for its keep and there would be cash for extra rides. He had said nothing to Gwyn, but only because his stepfather was ill and Martin himself had been so busy that he had forgotten.

Now there would be trouble.

There would be extra work to do; the pony had to be fed, groomed, and exercised. Martin hadn't realized just how much time was spent in caring for all the animals.

He and Anna Wyn had raced from job to job and even now, at eight o'clock, they hadn't finished. There was more to do. The ponies hadn't been shut in for the night, nor had they had their last feed. The bucket of water for Charlotte waited by the kitchen door. He thought wearily of the trek across the yard to the far end of the sanctuary field where she had her sty.

Gwyn stared at his daughter.

"What pony? I said no more ponies."

"It's Tag's." Martin was suddenly afraid of his stepfather. "He's given it to us, to keep at livery and use on the sanctuary. He got fed up with it."

"Who said we'd take it? Who's going to do all the extra work?"

Martin looked at Blue, and swallowed. If only he'd thought. He was always doing something wrong.

"They're paying for it. I didn't think it would matter."

"Time, boy. Time." Gwyn's eyes were angry. His wife brought him his medicine. He drank it, his face wry. "Another responsibility for Anna Wyn. You don't do much to help, do you?"

The quiet bitter voice was worse than any yell.

He stood up, holding on to the edge of the table, and his eyes stared into Martin's, revealing his fury.

"I say what happens here, and don't you forget it. If the pony stays, you look after it. You feed it. You groom it. There's enough to do when we're

47

all fit, and now look at us . . . heaven only knows when I'm going to be able to do a day's work again. You don't do a hand's turn and if you do, you mess it up. All you ever do is slope off with that dog."

It wasn't fair. Martin was exhausted. He had done his best all day, and now they accused him of not helping. He had worked nonstop from six that morning. He ate breakfast standing and at lunchtime had not even stopped to eat, grabbing a sandwich as he went across the fields to check on the troughs. Nobody ever gave him credit for anything he did.

The day someone said "Well done, Martin," he'd die of shock. Anyone else would have had a few days rest after being ill, but as soon as he was on his feet he had to go out in the cold and the wet and slave for them.

He whistled to Blue, and slammed out of the door. Anna Wyn could finish on her own. She might have said he'd worked beside her all day, and not even taken ten minutes off.

"Getting too big for his boots," he heard Gwyn say. "The boy's useless." He waited outside the door to see if his mother would defend him, but the room was silent. Defeated, he went upstairs, taking the dog with him, although that was forbidden. He tossed on his bed, unable to sleep, listening to Blue's breathing. He wasn't going to stand it any more. Nobody wanted him.

He was tired of being treated like a child but

expected to do a man's work around the place. His mother was always scolding him, too.

"Pick that up. Put that away. How on earth did you get your rugby kit into that state? Go and do your homework. Have you fed Blue?"

He hated all of them.

Tomorrow, he'd show them. Maybe they'd be sorry and maybe they wouldn't. He just didn't care. Outside his window an owl hooted, and one of the owls in the sanctuary answered it. That would be Olly, who had only one eye and half a wing.

Martin lay awake for a long time, making plans. It was well after midnight before he fell asleep.

The shrill alarm sounded much too soon, and for a moment he was tempted to change his mind. But not for long. Resentment flared. His stepfather never gave him credit for anything. Nor did anyone else. The livery money and the charges for rides would more than make up for the extra work. Why couldn't they see that?

He dressed, packed his rucksack, and flicked his finger to Blue, who followed him, astounded at being up and about before anyone else was stirring.

He crept downstairs, his shoes in his hand, and into the kitchen where a sleepy cat lifted and head and yawned at him. There were pasties in the refrigerator. He took four of them, and a bag of rolls. He had very little money. Maybe someone would give him a job helping on another farm.

He was never coming back, any way. Not ever. Maybe they would be sorry, but he knew they'd all be glad.

He opened the door and went out into the early dawn, creeping across the yard. The dark house slept behind him. The first pale glow of the sun shone on the dewdrops on bushes which as yet had no colour, and were as grey as the sky.

He was raw with misery, but now he was doing something about it.

Chapter 6

Martin slipped out of the farmyard, anxious not to disturb Mervyn's dogs. He didn't want one single bark to betray his presence. Blue, close beside him, sensed his urgency, and padded softly, a shadow at his master's heels.

It was very dark. The grass was crisp and brittle under their feet. A faint shimmer in the air glowed on hedge and grass. Martin dared not use a torch. Gwyn might be well enough to get up at any minute, and see the light and come to investigate.

Anna Wyn would have to work alone. She'd be sorry when she realized how much Martin had done the day before. He was bitter and angry. Blue nosed the boy's hand.

A niggle of guilt fought its way into Martin's mind, but he was determined to leave his step-family for ever. They could starve, for all he cared. As he walked, his mood changed again, and he felt desolate. Nobody would bother about him. They probably wouldn't even bother to tell the police if he didn't come back. Just say "Good riddance," and get on with their lives, behaving as if he had never existed.

Anna Wyn's angry voice rang in his mind.

"We wouldn't be in this state if we didn't have to keep them too. She's not my mother; and he's not my brother."

Well, now they'd have one less mouth to feed. He thought of Gwyn's words the night before, and of his mother sitting there, accepting them, saying nothing. He wished he'd never been born. His own father hadn't wanted him. Now his mother didn't either.

He watched the sun rise red in a sky streaked with sulphur yellow clouds. The mountains on the mainland were hidden. The light strengthened, but the sun was soon only a memory and the sky dark. Bad weather was coming.

Martin leaned against the wall and ate one of his pasties, sharing it with Blue. He had put in a pack of dog biscuits. His mother would be angry because he had taken food, but she'd be glad he'd gone. One of her problems solved.

He needed to be hidden and move at night, or someone would see him. There was a ruined church in the woods beyond Tag's family's caravan field. There were also caves, left from old mine workings. He could hide in the ruins, or in the old mines. Taid said they were haunted, and Martin shivered.

The darkening sky was uncanny, lit by an eerie glow. There was definitely a storm brewing. The world had narrowed to a few fields, and the woods on the horizon. Blue was anxious, his tail held low, his eyes worried, as he sensed his master's mood.

A ferocious wind screamed out of the sky, hurling itself across waves that hissed and broke in a smother of foam. The trees bent as if made of paper. Walking was a battle. Two tiles whirled out of the air, flung from the roof of a cottage that lay empty, a "for sale" notice at the gate. Martin bent his head against its blast.

Bent double, barely able to see, Martin heard the crack as a branch broke from a nearby tree, crashing to the ground. Lightning flared across the sky and thunder roared, echoing from the mountains.

He held Blue's leash tightly, his hand reassuring the dog, whose ears were flat as he stared wild-eyed at a world gone mad. A sudden torrent soaked them both within moments.

If he could lie against the wall he might have shelter. But it might be blown down by the wind and kill them both.

The lane was bordered by a wide grass verge, onto which they wandered. Martin did not see the hole. He caught his foot, tripped, fell heavily, and lay still, feeling sick. Rain and wind, thunder and lightning combined to convince his half-dazed mind that he was being punished for running away.

The dog lay down beside him and licked his face.

Martin knew how stupid he had been. No-one knew where he had gone. He might not be found for days. He had never been down this lane before and had no idea where it led. Perhaps there was a house, but he knew as soon as he tried to stand that he couldn't walk. He must have broken his ankle.

It served him right. He would lie there for ever. Nobody knew where he had gone. No one would come to look for him.

The pain unnerved him, and the rain, soaking him, warned him that he could die here of exposure. So many mountain deaths were not due to injury at all, but to lying in wind and rain, gradually chilling.

Blue licked his face and nudged him with an urgent paw, as if trying to bring his master back to reality.

If he died, it wouldn't be fair to Blue. They'd put him to sleep. Nobody wanted him either. The thought needled Martin into trying to make some effort, any effort, to rescue himself. Nobody else would come.

He tried to move, to crawl, to lever himself along, but the pain swamped every other feeling and he dropped back to the ground, knowing that no misery he had ever endured before was half as bad as this.

The coast was near. He could hear the thudding of the waves against the shore, and the rain tasted of salt.

Maybe he could crawl.

That was agonizing and very slow. His leg hurt abominably. He had never imagined such pain. He lay, clutching the dog, thankful for the breathing body and the tongue that caressed his hand at intervals.

Then came regret. He ought to have stayed and looked after the pony. It was his fault Caley was there. He thought of Anna Wyn, struggling on her own to do the chores that had taken the two of them more than twelve hours, working nonstop. His mother was in no fit state to help and Gwyn was really ill. Suppose he got up and tried to help and had a heart attack?

It would be Martin's fault.

He was as stupid as Tag and he hadn't thought anyone else could be that stupid.

He lay, feeling too sick to worry any more, knowing that he was chilling.

He closed his eyes and drifted between despair and agony, knowing that this was the end. He was so wet that he felt he was part of a river; and so cold that he knew he could never be warm again. Maybe if he slept death would come fast and painlessly; not as it was coming now, with every breath searing his chest.

He couldn't stand. The sky was whirling above him.

He gripped his dog, and lay conscious of the wet grass against his face, and the smell of damp earth.

Then came another noise. A swirl and roar and crash, a slow seeping that came over his feet, and receded again. He twisted his head. The lane was near the sea. Too near. The wild white waves were crashing over the low wall, hiding the far edge of the verge, creeping towards him. The sea!

The sea had come in for three miles, only two years ago, drowning a whole housing estate under water. The Sea Zoo had been islanded by water that day. The road that led to it vanished under the waves.

If he stayed here, he would drown.

Desperately, he began to claw his way across the ground towards the road. Thistles tore at his hands. Nettles stung his face. Sharp stones bit into his skin. If only he had stayed at home. If only he had not fallen . . . if only someone would come.

He was alone in a desolate lane, without a house or person in sight. No cars would come along here now. He buried his head in Blue's fur, and felt the remorseless creep of the seeking waves, up to his knees, up to his thighs, and soon, over his face.

Chapter 7

Martin jumped when Blue barked.

"Hey. Hey. What have we here?"

The man staring down at him was young. He wore a neat short beard. Dark hair travelled down his cheeks and almost entirely hid his face. He took off his jacket and put it round Martin. "Hurt? can you stand?"

"My ankle," Martin said. "I can't move. I tried."

His rescuer sensed the despair.

Strong arms went round his body, holding him under the armpits, lifting him from the ground.

"Come on. Never give up. Nothing's hopeless. It's only your leg that's damaged; not your head. That might be a disaster."

The stranger was a big man, and he seemed to

have enough strength and energy for two. He went on talking.

"Luck's on your side. It's over a year since I walked down this lane. Doubt if anyone else does from Sunday to Sunday. It's a dead end."

Martin was moving in a daze, water dripping from him. His hair lay wet across his head, and rain ran into his eyes. He felt dizzy and sick.

"Try hopping," the man said. "My cottage is a little way along the road; if we can get you there . . . if the wind doesn't see us both flat on the ground. Never known a gale like this. Or such thunder," he added as another peal rumbled on and on overhead. "The gods of war are fighting one another."

Martin dropped Blue's lead, but the dog followed, desperate not to be left alone. They were moving at a crawl, each step an agony. The wind took away all breath. Even the stranger, who loved talking, had no words to say.

The rain eased. They stopped several times for Martin to lean against the wall. Hop and stop. Hop and stop. He was thankful for the strong arms that held him up. Without them he would have fallen.

The cottage was tiny, two rooms and leanto sheds for both kitchen and bathroom. Bright with colour, the white walls were covered with pictures of animals. Badger and fox, deer and seal, herds of oryx and a multitude of cats that played and jumped or sat watching with enigmatic eyes.

There were shelves filled with wooden animals.

A bull, its head lowered, seemed to charge a seal. A bear, sitting up with a ball balanced on its paw, watched a leaping jaguar.

Martin, lying on a settee that almost filled the room, took a deep breath. The raging wind screamed round the cottage, alarming Blue, who crept to Martin's side and thrust his head into the boy's hand.

He had been stripped of his wet clothes as if he were a tiny boy again, towelled dry, and wrapped in warm blankets. The shivering eased, and he was aware of knifing pain. He had never known anything hurt so much as his damaged leg. His rescuer was filling a mug from the kettle on the little stove. He opened the doors so that the glow shone into the room.

"It gets too hot at times in summer," he said. "But I don't have anything else for cooking, so it's always on. Just what we need today."

Blue planted himself on a brilliantly coloured rag rug.

"I'm Daft Dannie," the man said. Martin stared at him, suddenly afraid, remembering stories he had heard about this particular character.

"Know why they call me daft?"

Martin shook his head.

"Because I go on making wooden animals and painting pictures and never sell any of them, unless I like the person I'm selling to. Don't want just anyone to have them. They need good homes, just as real animals do."

He handed the mug to Martin.

"Drink it up. I've put a couple of aspirins in. Take away some of the pain. Let's have a look at the damage."

As he moved, Martin was suddenly aware that Dannie walked in an odd way, as if his leg wouldn't bend.

"My peg-leg doesn't help the stories that go round," Dannie said. "Superstitious lot round here. Actually I had an argument with a shell in the Falklands war; the shell won and they fitted me up with a new leg. Not much I can't do, though." He lifted Martin gently, and put cushions behind his back and held the mug to his lips.

"I thought the end of the world had come when they took my leg off. Smile, they said and I did, though I screamed inside. And then I learned that there is still a life to be lived and enjoyed. I could be much worse off than I am. You have to make the best of whatever happens."

Martin, expecting to taste coffee, tasted soup. He swallowed, revelling in the glow of warmth that flooded his body. A few minutes before, he had thought he would die. Now he was comfortable and cosseted, and Dannie was behaving as if he had known Martin for ever.

The big man laughed. "You won't lose your leg. Don't worry. Breaks and tears heal. Shells destroy and wartime injuries are far worse than anything like this. Let's take a look at it."

He lifted the blankets.

Martin looked at his foot. Dannie had left the sock on it, when he undressed him, not wanting to hurt Martin more than he need. He bent down and cut the sock off, exposing a bruised mass.

"Arnica cream. That's a sprain, not a break, I'll guarantee. You were lucky. Hurts nearly as much, but you'll soon be moving again. What on earth were you doing up here in this weather?"

"Running away," Martin said, surprising himself, but Dannie invited confidences.

"Daft day to choose. Must be dafter than I am. Where are your folks? Dad got up your nose? I remember that feeling. My own dad could make me want to leave home for ever at times. Mind you, I usually deserved all I got."

He laughed, and drank his own soup from a blue mug patterned with geese.

"He's not my dad. He's my stepfather. My mother married again. My own dad ran out on us, and left us when I was five." Martin's teeth began to chatter again.

Dannie walked out of the room, and came back carrying another thick blanket.

"Shock. Always makes you cold. Better get you warm," he said. "Lie still. They'll have to come for you. I don't have a car. Do they know you left home? Leave a note for them?"

"No. I just went."

"Do you usually walk your dog this early?"

Martin nodded. "No need to tell them different. Never any point in running headfirst into trouble when you can avoid it. Half the art of war; get yourself out of danger, and keep your head down. Only sometimes you can't avoid the flak."

"Why did you come and live here?" Martin asked, not wanting to answer any more questions.

"My parents bought this as a holiday cottage. When they died I sold their house which was far too big for me, and came here. I can live on nothing. Keep a few chickens; give me eggs and table birds. Shoot a few rabbits, where there's no questions asked."

He perched on the edge of the table, grabbing a chocolate biscuit from a round tin, and throwing another to Martin. Blue caught it and Dannie laughed and tossed a second, this time too high for the dog to reach. He seemed to move faster than anyone Martin knew, in spite of his artificial leg.

He also talked faster.

"Grow my own vegetables. I can do odd jobs. People are always grateful for a hand when they need it, even if it is Daft Dannie. Mostly I do it for free; so long as I can eat and pay what's needed, who wants more?"

He laughed, as if life were an enormous joke. "I'm lucky, though thousands wouldn't agree. I don't want gourmet meals and fast cars and city sights. I hate crowds. Here, there are the mountains and the sky at night; the birds flying over. The geese in winter; the swans, their wings beating. I've the whole world to play with."

Martin drank. The soup's warmth flooded his

body and he began to feel much better even though his ankle throbbed as much as ever.

"Where's this farm of yours?" Dannie asked.

"Bryn Gwynt."

Dannie grinned.

"Well, well, everything comes to he who waits. Pretty little stepsister, isn't there?"

Martin had never thought of either of his stepsisters as pretty.

"Good man, your stepfather. You're lucky. Your mother might have done much worse for you. Time I had a change from painting and carving. There's plenty to sell if I find the right customers. I reckon you did your family a good turn when you rushed off this morning."

An immense black cat walked into the room, and stared with angry green eyes at Blue. Blue, used to cats, watched with interest as the animal passed him, and then, deciding the dog was no threat, jumped to his master's knee and began to purr at the top of a very considerable voice.

"Funny old world," Dannie said, his voice dreamy. "Often we get upset over things that aren't real to anyone but us. We're sure people don't like us, when actually they're so busy they don't have time to think."

Martin felt as if life had whisked him into another dimension.

"Ever hear from your own dad?" Dannie asked. For some reason, Martin did not resent the question.

"No. His mother writes to us though. He married again and went to live in Australia. He's got two little girls."

"Older and more sense by then," Dannie sighed. "I nearly married when I was twenty-one." He laughed again. "All of four years ago. Thought the world would end if I didn't. She was lovely, and only seventeen, but I didn't want to wait for her."

He stroked the cat and looked back into the past. "She wouldn't say yes and she wouldn't say no. I know now she was much too young, but I didn't know that then. It would have been a disaster. Seemed like the worst luck in the world then, but it wasn't."

"What happened?"

"The Falklands happened. I'd joined the Army just before I met her. When I came back I'd grown up; and she hadn't. She was just a silly little girl with no thought in her head except for clothes and dancing; you can't dance with a one-legged man. I can do most things, as I said, but not that." Dannie put the cat on the floor. It promptly jumped on to the settee and cuddled down beside Martin. Blue came over and nosed it, jealous. It opened one green eye, put out a lazy paw and pushed at him, claws sheathed.

"If your stepfather is still ill, is there anyone there who can drive? It's actually only about three miles."

"Anna Wyn. She'll be busy, though."

"I'll come back with you. You'd be surprised

the amount of work I can get through in a day. Look forward to it. Nice to work with animals again. I always wanted to. That's why I work out my feelings in paint and wood. There's something wrong with people who don't like animals, I think. Like a sense missing. The world will end the day the last four-legged creature dies, and the last bird falls from the sky. Man wasn't meant to exist in a sterile environment."

Martin, looking at the menagerie, suddenly remembered his Noah's Ark. Perhaps Dannie could make some animals; could help him with that. It would make the accident worthwhile, almost.

The phone box must have been some way away. Dannie had only been back about five minutes when the Land Rover drew up to the door.

"You are a hopeless ass," said Anna Wyn, as soon as she saw Martin. "Trust you to sprain an ankle when everyone else is ill." But she sounded more concerned than angry.

"It was Kismet," Dannie said laughing. "Written in the stars. You need me more than you need Martin right now. I can do twice his work. My strength is as the strength of ten because my heart is pure. He's done you a good turn."

Anna Wyn laughed.

"OK, Sir Galahad. The Pritchards said you're as mad as a March Hare." She grinned at him. "They were obviously right. Come on, there's a power of work waiting at home and we'd better get Martin back. I suppose he ought to have that ankle X-rayed."

"Ask Tom Pritchard to take him. He owes you for young Tag's life two years back. Says he's never been able to repay Martin."

"We manage," Anna Wyn said. "Don't like asking favours."

"We need each other." Dannie had almost lifted Martin out of the house and into the Land Rover. Blue jumped up and settled on the floor. "I help you; you help me. That's the way the world goes round."

"And what do I do to help you?" Anna Wyn asked, as she started the engine.

"That," said Dannie, smiling, "would be telling."

Martin, looking at him, wondered if he knew more than Anna Wyn about his rescuer.

Chapter 8

Tom Pritchard was only too pleased to take Martin to hospital, where the X-ray confirmed that his ankle was sprained. Bandaged and irritable, he sat in the big chair in the kitchen later that day, watching his mother unpack his rucksack.

She laid the pasties and the dog biscuits on the table, and his change of clothes, and spare jersey and pyjamas. Gwyn, who had got up that morning for the first time since his illness, had soon given up and returned to bed. Anna Wyn and Dannie were busy with the animals.

"Why?" she asked.

"Nobody wants me, and I never do anything right."

He stroked Blue's head, fondling the dog's soft ears, feeling that this was the only creature in the world that understood him.

"You are an idiot sometimes, Martin." Leah slammed down the rucksack on to the floor as if it had suddenly bitten her. "Do you really think we wouldn't have cared?"

"I never expected to fall and hurt myself. I didn't think you wanted me. I was going to pretend to be sixteen and get a job . . . maybe a stable lad at Newmarket." He had only just thought of that, but he was determined not to give in easily. Leah looked at him, exasperated.

"You should have asked Gwyn about Caley," she said. "He's afraid you'll fill the place with waifs and strays, too. It's bad enough with Anna Wyn. She's never learned to say no. We can't do with two of you."

"I didn't think of the work, only the money," Martin eased his leg, trying to relieve the throbbing pain. "There ought to be a good profit on rides if we have him here all week."

"We need a fortune, not a few extra pounds each week. Gwyn was angry because he felt ill, as well as being desperately worried."

Blue, bothered by the atmosphere in the room, thrust his head hard against her knee and Leah reached down and stroked him.

"Dai took the three barren ewes to market for us. Gwyn paid eighty pounds for each of them. Do you know what he got?"

Martin shook his head.

"Three pounds each. We need more money

desperately. As it is we have to borrow from the bank and they don't go on lending for ever. The grass in the river fields has been under water so much this summer that we've had to feed hay. The price of that has hit the roof, and we need more all the time."

She thrust a mug of coffee into Martin's hands, and slammed down a plate on the table as if she hated it. He looked at the slice of cake and the scone, and knew his mother was trying to say he was forgiven, at least by her.

"You never tell me anything," Martin said. "How am I supposed to know?"

"When are you here to listen? It takes two people to have a conversation, son. You're either out with the dog, or away with some scheme of your own, and you so often resent everything we say to you."

She put the pasties in the refrigerator, and shut the door with a bang. She stood the dog biscuit packet back on the shelf. Blue watched her with eager eyes, hoping food might come his way, but she walked out of the room, leaving Martin feeling so utterly miserable that he was afraid he would cry.

Firelight glinted on the plates on the dresser. Tiny flames danced in Spider's green eyes, as he crouched on his high perch. The room drifted out of focus and Martin slept, wakening to the sound of Dannie's riotous laugh as he came through the door.

"Hey, soldier," he said. "Been sleeping? Be on your feet in no time." He took the kettle and two mugs that were standing on the dresser, the coffee jar beside them, behaving as if he belonged. "Anna Wyn told me to come in and make a drink. Want one?"

Martin nodded. Glancing at the clock he found he had been asleep for nearly two hours. His ankle was on fire.

"I've been looking at the Sanctuary. It's more like a hospital than an animal park at present with all those invalids. Need more attractions if we're to get people away from the other places on the island. I've elected Dannie Kent as adviser."

He grinned at Martin, and seated himself astride a chair, his arms leaning on its back. "I've been out of circulation too long. Tired of my own company. There's scope here for lots of ideas. That little playground has immense possiblities. I could do something I always wanted to do. Hadn't thought of doing it with children though."

"What's that?"

"Use this as the base for an outward bound school for tinies. Horse riding; assault course. I never had any land before. If I can do it here, then I can work for your dad for nothing, and he does need help."

And how will that help us? Martin wondered, feeling too wretched to see any future for anyone. If Dannie did all the things he was planning there'd be no time for him to help round the farm.

"Come on, soldier. Cheer up. You might have broken your neck and be dead. You might have cracked your skull, and never regained your wits. I might not have found you. You might have been found by someone who didn't know what to do or how to help you."

"And I might have been trampled by a mad bull," Martin said, determined to be unco-operative. He stared at Dannie and shivered suddenly. He nearly had been trampled by a mad bull. He'd forgotten Hero.

He began to feel out of breath, just listening. He had never met anyone with so much energy before. The room vibrated. Dannie put three spoonsful of sugar in his cup and stirred it vigorously.

"But you weren't, and I did find you. I told you that it was all meant to happen . . . that I should meet you, come here, and find myself a new job."

"We can't afford you," Martin said.

"I don't need the money. I do need to be with people and have a new interest. It's lonely working by yourself all day. Your mother can sell the things I make in the shop and take commission."

In spite of his irritation Martin thought that maybe Dannie would be fun.

"You'd have to ask . . . "

"Your stepfather. Yes, I know. I hope he'll jump at it, especially now, with Mervyn's farm to help with as well."

"How did you know about that?"

71

"No secrets in a village. I do talk to people. Even drop in for a drink at *The Setters* now and then. I have to eat and food comes from shops and people love to chat."

Anna Wyn's sudden wail startled both of them. Dannie raced outside, leaving Martin staring after him. He felt as if he had been hit by a series of hammer blows. The big man spilled over with excitement and never seemed to simmer down.

He was very quiet when he came back into the room, carrying the little ginger cat. She lay, as if dead, in his arms.

"She was in the lane, and ran towards the gate, across the road," Anna Wyn said. "The car never even stopped; went right over her."

"She isn't dead. But she's badly hurt. Means a trip to the vet." Dannie laid her gently on the table. Blood stained her side, and her eyes were closed, but Martin could see that she was still breathing.

"We'll have to find her kittens." Anna Wyn sounded desolate.

Leah, coming back into the room, took one look and tightened her lips. Martin could read his mother's mind. Another vet bill, and it wouldn't be a small one. Worry began to niggle. What would they all do if they couldn't manage? Where would they go?"

"I'll look for the kittens," Dannie said. "They're in the barn?"

Anna Wyn nodded. "I haven't even heard them. I think they're in the roof."

"They'll make enough noise when they're hungry. She won't be able to feed them even if she does recover; or at least not for days and then her milk'll probably have dried up. Need some kitten milk and something to feed them with."

Anna Wyn put the cat in the wire carrying cage, and went out as Leah rang the vet to tell them she was on her way.

Taid appeared suddenly in the doorway, reminding Martin of a disreputable genii. The old man walked slowly across to the table and sat down, easing himself painfully. His clothes seemed to be too large for him. He huddled inside them, as if desperate to keep warm.

Leah handed him a mug of coffee and he cradled it in his hands.

"Be glad when the sun gets some heat," he said. He looked at Martin. "That ankle may seem like a bit of bad luck. But Gwyn says you're clever with sums and maybe you can help with the farm books while you're laid up. Glad it wasn't any worse, Bach. That lane is under water every time a sea gale blows."

Martin felt stupid. He hadn't known. He ought to learn about the place he lived in, or he'd get into more trouble.

"Meanwhile, who does the work round here?" Taid asked. "Gwyn laid up, Martin out of action . . ."

"The new help." Dannie erupted into the room, his jersey pouched in front of him, active with small mewing creatures. "I can do two mens' work on one day . . . I was brought up on a farm. Tell me what needs doing and I'll do it."

"Daft Dannie," said Taid, his eyes astonished. "They said you never come out of hiding. Well, well . . . "

"Never believe what you're told." Dannie's laugh made them all smile in spite of their feelings of misery.

"We can't repay you in any way." Leah stroked one of the kittens thoughtfully.

"Oh, yes you can. I need a family. My parents are dead, and my sister busy with husband and two children, and she doesn't live near. It would give me something more to do than sitting at home painting or carving."

He picked up the blanket from Blue's bed and put it on Martin's lap, then decanted the kittens carefully from his jersey. They sprawled, mewing pathetically.

"They're hungry," Dannie said. "You'll have to be mother. Give you something to do while you can't walk. Anna Wyn's bringing back some special milk from the vet. Taid can mix it. Doesn't take a lot of energy." He grinned at the old man. "Meanwhile I'd better see to the ponies."

"I wonder if he ever shuts a door." Leah watched Dannie hurtle across the yard as if chased by ravening monsters.

"Organize us all," Taid said. He laughed. "We need a bit of life round here, and he'll provide it, and more."

"He's like a tornado," Martin said, as one of the tiny kittens seized his finger and tried to suck. He stared down at them. "I've never met anyone like him before."

"Maybe just as well," his mother said. "Just listening to him is exhausting. Too many like him and we'd all be worn out." She laughed, and Martin suddenly realized how rarely she did that now. "I think he could be good for all of us."

Martin felt the little bodies move against his hand. The tiny ears were cold. The minute transparent claws scrabbled at the blanket, and a constant fretful mewling came from each open mouth.

"They're very hungry indeed," Leah said. "I don't know if we can save them. It's never easy to rear baby animals, and kittens and puppies are among the most difficult." She had wrapped a hot water bottle inside a blanket, and lifted the kittens gently from Martin's lap and put them in a cardboard box.

Blue lay on the rug, watching. Spider jumped down from the top of the dresser. He spat at the dog as he passed, but he was determined to find out what was making the strange sounds. They triggered something deep in his brain, and worried him.

He walked towards the box. He stared inside, and then jumped in, settled himself down among the babies, and began to wash them with his rough tongue. Martin wondered if the babies were his. They were all ginger like their mother. Tomcats sometimes killed kittens, but Spider didn't seem to know that.

Blue lay with his nose on his paw, a curious look in his eyes as if he were faced with something beyond his understanding.

"That's one problem solved," Leah said. "I was afraid he might hurt them. He'll help keep them warm, and they'll be happier than if they were on their own."

Martin, looking down at the wriggling bodies that nestled up to the black and white cat, suddenly understood what motivated Anna Wyn. He now had responsibilities, and he knew, with fierce certainty, that he was going to do his very best to ensure these mites did not die.

Chapter 9

Martin felt crippled. He'd taken walking for granted for so long, and now he could only hobble with the help of a stick. Every step was painful and he only moved when necessary. Gwyn, coming wearily downstairs, gripped his stepson's shoulder.

"Bad luck, lad," he said. He laid a photograph album in Martin's lap. "Something to look at. The farm, and the girls when they were small, and some of our prize winning animals. Life was different, twenty years ago . . . even ten years ago . . . " He sighed.

Martin recognized it as a peace offering, perhaps even an apology.

Dilys brought him copies of *The Reader's Digest* to read. Dannie brought absurdities: a pink sugar mouse, a chocolate whale he'd bought at the Sea

Zoo, when he called in there to persuade them to give left over fish to the Sanctuary. He also brought one large prawn, and all the free literature he could lay his hands on. "Might get ideas from it. We need to advertise too," he said. Anna Wyn brought half a pound of nut chocolate which she left on the arm of his chair. Her face was pink with embarrassment.

Mervyn often sat with him, talking about his farm and the day that Hero escaped.

"You did well, boy," Gwyn said, hearing the tale for the first time. "Never realized . . . "

Tag visited, bringing games and jigsaws, and sat and chattered endlessly, so that Martin sometimes wished that he would be less enthusiastic about cheering up the invalid.

The kittens became a major source of interest over the next few days. Unable to walk, time passed slowly for Martin, but the kittens had to be fed every two hours. Taid slept by day so that he could feed them at night. When the old man came in in the evenings, Martin told him what had happened during the day: how each had fed, which sucked fast on the teat and which sucked slow.

Martin was startled to find that, by the time he had fed the kittens twice, they associated his hand with milk. Their eyes had opened, too, and Dannie reckoned they were about two weeks old.

As soon as Martin's hand reached into the box, the biggest kitten, who everyone nicknamed the Pirate, because of a white patch round one eye,

78

seized a finger and sucked. He was always the first to be fed, as he was by far the noisiest if left in the box.

Spider, taking his task of proxy father very seriously, was at first alarmed by the noise the kittens made at feeding time, but he quickly learned that it was hunger, not fear, that triggered them.

Not one of the five would feed unless cuddled first. The routine was always the same. Each kitten in turn swarmed up Martin's arm, clinging to his sweatshirt sleeve. Then it cuddled under his chin, rubbing against his skin, purring, an odd little rusty purr that, Martin thought, at first, meant they had a lung infection. Spider supervised this procedure from the table edge, watching intently.

Blue, at first astounded, grew used to the kittens being bottle-fed, and went to sleep. He couldn't understand why Dannie was walking him instead of Martin, and frowned in bewilderment as he watched his master's painful movements round the kitchen.

The kittens had names and personalities. The Pirate was boss of the litter, wanting most food and the warmest place in the box. He was the most mischievous, too, earning himself several paw slaps from Spider, who objected to kittens that bit his tail or tried to suck from his ear.

Little Sandy, the palest of the five, was timid, and needed a great deal of coaxing to drink at all. He cuddled round the tiny bottle that Dilys had borrowed from a breeder of Chihuahuas, and kept his eyes fixed on Martin with an unwinking stare.

Mew, the most plaintive of them, had four white paws and a white tip to her tail. She was always eager for her food, but seemed unable to understand what the teat was for. The start of her feed was always a struggle.

Slow had a white tip to his tail and a small white bib. He was deeper in colour than the others, but he was always last. He was jostled away from the warmth, and pushed away from Martin's hand. The Pirate would have had two feeds if he could have managed it, and he seemed determined that Slow should have none.

Little Pi made all of them laugh. Dilys was sure that if Pi had been a girl she would have been prim and proper, always immaculate. She was the first to wash herself, and once she had discovered washing she never seemed to stop. In the nest, she washed any kitten that came up against her.

One morning, when she was nearly five weeks old, she washed Blue's head so diligently that his fur was soaked. He was now used to kittens climbing all over him, or even jumping at one another on his back. When he was tired of them he shook them off, and stalked across the room to find a place safe from small fry.

He and Spider had a truce. Spider didn't hiss at Blue so long as Blue didn't give chase.

Ginger spent three weeks in the hospital as everyone felt it better to keep her away from her kittens until she was healed and strong again. Her pelvis was broken, her jaw badly damaged, and she had a long gash on her side, which became infected.

"We can't get rid of them," Dilys said, coming home one evening, and taking over the feed for Martin. The kittens were just beginning to learn to eat solid food. Spider, to everyone's surprise, had taught them all about litter trays, and led a small procession to squat on the peat.

When they were six weeks old and feeding themselves, Anna Wyn took them across to the park, where they proved a major attraction. More of an attraction than she had thought as by the end of the first week four had been found new homes, and only the Pirate was left.

He took great pleasure in leaping into the rabbit run and pretending the rabbits were cats. Blackie, an immense buck, soon taught him a lesson. Kicked and sorry for himself, he crept to Anna Wyn, and after that stayed close to her, following her around like a small dog wherever she went.

He learned to dodge Arnold the turkey, who didn't like cats, and to keep out of the way of the small goats' bucking hooves.

Lola gave birth to sixteen little pigs. Ten of them, usefully, would grow into breeding sows. Anna Wyn supervised the birth. Martin wished he had been there, but he couldn't manage to stand for long.

His ankle was mending, but he couldn't walk

on it yet, and was still at home when school ended.

Dannie took the children for their rides on Caley and soon no one could remember what life had been like without him.

Gwyn, busier than ever, had no time for anyone. Martin woke one morning to find a sheet of paper beside him. He was still sleeping on the big kitchen windowseat, as the stairs were too difficult to climb without a great deal of pain.

He stared at it.

"You now have a number of new responsibilities. These are yours, and you need to find the money to feed them. Blue. Lola and her babies and Caley. You can have the livery money, which should help cover food and hopefully the blacksmith as his hooves will need trimming regularly. If he goes out on the road he must be shod. You can keep them as long as you pay for them."

Martin took his stick and limped out into the yard.

Dannie paused on his way to the Sanctuary with a barrow full of feed for the various animals. "How about that Noah's Ark? Want me to get it here so that we can start? We could keep it in the big barn until it's ready to go on site."

Martin looked at the sty where Lola had her babies, at Caley, tethered at the edge of the park, waiting for rides, and at Blue, who was stretched out by his feet. Mervyn and his dogs had gone back to the farm, which was now for sale. Taid, weary and aching, rarely moved from his arm chair these days.

Martin held out Gwyn's letter.

"Fair enough," Dannie said. "Have to be clever, won't we? Find a way you can earn enough to keep them till those little pigs are big enough to sell. Tom Pritchard says you're a wizard with figures. So how about thinking of a way of making some figures to be a wizard with?"

The day stretched in front of him. He could manage to walk as far as the Sanctuary and help Anna Wyn, so long as he sat at the table. He could take the money, and maybe while he was working he would come up with a useful idea. There was so much they could do to improve the place, but ideas were no use unless there was money to back them.

It was a bright day, a blue day, with sunshine spilling over the hills. Anna Wyn vacated her place with a sigh of relief, as someone had brought in a seagull covered in oil and she wanted to bath him.

There were more visitors than they had had in one day before. Dannie soon had to fetch cups of tea and sandwiches and sort out ice creams. No one ever wanted those that were easy to find. Each order meant an exploration, as the little refrigerator was far too small and everything was in disorganized piles.

Martin looked around him. They needed more

display shelves. They needed more goods to sell. They needed to think. They needed to organise. They needed time.

If only he could find some buried treasure. Or discover that one of Gwyn's pictures was worth a fortune. He couldn't even take a job when he could barely hobble. He had torn a ligament in his ankle, and he began to wonder if he would ever be able to walk properly again.

Money. No wonder everyone worried about it. How much did it cost to feed Lola and her babies? How much to feed Caley? It cost £4 a week to feed Blue, and that took all his pocket money.

Around three o'clock there was a lull. Anna Wyn brought the damp seagull into the shop, and put him in a cage, where he sat in huddled misery. Dannie followed her in.

"A baby herring gull," she said. She took fish from the refrigerator, and cut it into pieces which she dropped into the cage. The bird looked at it, indifferent.

"I think he'll survive," she said. "Not too much oil and he's otherwise healthy."

She made coffee for the three of them, and brought out sandwiches. There were children playing in the sandpit, children on the swings, and children in the rabbit pen. Caley, saddled, was tethered to the rail outside the shop. It was some time before Martin realized the pony had eaten every pansy in the tub that Taid had put to brighten the grass.

He hoped no-one else would notice.

There was a noise from the cage. The seagull had begun to peck at the fish.

Martin looked up as a small boy came towards them, his face miserable. His mother walked behind them. The child held out a bleeding finger.

Trouble. How had he done that? Would they be blamed?

"Tell them what I told you to say," the child's mother said.

"Please do you have some plaster? It was my own fault. The rat bit me. The notice on the cage said 'Don't put your fingers in this cage,' and I wondered why, and I did!"

"And now he knows," his mother said. She laughed and ruffled the boy's hair. "He's impossible. I hope it will teach him a lesson, but he's not the kind of child that learns."

Like me, Martin thought, remembering the problems he had had with the animals when he first came to the farm. But he had learned, and maybe this boy would too.

Dannie grinned. He took the child into the cloakroom. He washed the bite, and dressed it with antiseptic cream and a bandage. He brought him back to the shop. Martin, looking through the entrance into the yard, had been watching cars pass down the lane, willing them to turn in at the gate, but very few did.

"Better get him an anti-tetanus injection," Dannie said. "I hope when you go to the zoo you won't want to see what will happen if you try to stroke a tiger. You might get a bad shock. Little animals get frightened; that's when they bite. Come to that," he added, "even big animals can get scared. We have to be careful, all the time."

Martin thought of the bull. Had he been scared, or just plain mean?

"The least we can do is give you a donation towards the cost of the animals," the mother said, putting a five pound note in the tin. "It really wasn't the rat's fault at all."

Anna Wyn watched them go and sighed.

"That means that we'll have to take Silas out of the park. It's a pity as he's a charmer. I've never known him even try to bite before. He'll be afraid of all boys now, and some other child might have the same silly idea. Can't they read?"

"Don't want to," Dannie said. "Tell a boy not to do something and ten to one he'll try it.

"There was a sudden squeal of rage, followed by a demented bray.

"That's Maggie and Skippy. What now?" Anna Wyn asked, as she ran towards the ponies. Dannie followed her, and Martin, cursing his slowness, limped after them.

A small group of children stood near, staring. The gates of both the pony enclosure and the donkey enclosure were open.

"The pony kicked the donkey. He's fallen into the guinea pig pit," one of the children said.

"Who opened the gate?"

"Simon. He's gone," one of the children said.

Dannie and Anna Wyn walked over to the guinea pig enclosure, Martin hobbling behind them. The little animals were standing on the big mound, looking in fascination into the dry moat that prevented their escape.

Skippy the donkey lay there on his back, struggling desperately. Maggie, her foal due any day, grazed smugly, as if pleased that she had rid herself of a rival that she hated. Everyone took the greatest care to keep the two apart.

"What in the world do we do to get him out of there?" Anna Wyn asked.

Nobody had the slightest idea. Even if Skippy righted himself, there was no way he could climb the ditch and the wall, and if he clambered up the mound, he most certainly couldn't jump out.

Martin, sitting on the edge of the wall, racked his brain frantically, trying to suggest possibilities. They had more than enough to do without silly incidents like this.

There was an imperative ring from the bell in the shop. Anna Wyn turned her head.

"Wouldn't you know it?" she said. "Our first coachload this summer has come in. Now what do we do?"

Chapter 10

Martin could at least think. He couldn't deal with the donkey, but he could help with the coach tour. He still had his tongue. He grinned at himself.

"Dannie'll have to cope with Skippy. I can't do much here, but I can manage in the shop."

"I'll get Skippy on his legs, and find some hay. The Guinea pigs will have to be shut in in case he treads on them. Whoops, there they go. Can't move him till we close. Off with you and cope."

As always, when he was bothered or busy, Dannie battered them with words.

Martin laglegged as fast as he could after Anna Wyn, who managed a smile as she arrived although she was out of breath.

"Sorry, the donkey just fell in the guinea pig pit,"

she said, earning herself an astounded glance from an elderly man whose grey beard poked out at an amazing angle from his chin.

"Is there a discount for coach parties?"

Anna Wyn stared at him. The subject had never arisen before. She began to do hurried sums in her head, but Martin was before her.

"Ten percent," he said, that being the easiest figure to deal with unexpectedly. "How many of you are there?"

"Forty."

Anna Wyn was busy multiplying £1.50 by 40 and then taking off 10%. Martin was equally busy multiplying £1.35p by 40, and came up with the answer while his stepsister was still struggling.

"That will be fifty-four pounds," he said.

It was more than they had ever taken in one afternoon. Martin was converting it into meal worms and pigfood as he put the money safely in the cash tin.

The little shop was so full that there seemed to be far more than 40 people.

"Martin," Anna Wyn said, as they went through into the park, "children are only sixty pence each and there are ten children there; we owe them money. What's ten percent of sixty pence? I wish it wasn't all so complicated."

"Ten times eighty-one pence."

"Are you sure?"

"Ten percent off one pound fifty is one pound thirty-five. Ten percent off sixty is fifty-four. One pound thirty five less fifty-four is eighty-one. We owe them eight pounds and ten pence. Right?"

"If you say so." Anna Wyn seemed mesmerized. She hated doing arithmetic.

Martin took the money out of the cash box, feeling deprived, and went in search of the elderly gentleman who had given him the cash.

Dannie had already shut in the guinea pigs, and helped Skippy struggle onto his legs inside the enclosure. The donkey, delighted at an extra meal, was placidly munching a pile of hay. Dannie was already acting as Guide.

"I'm sorry. I forgot that children are half price," Martin said, as he handed over the change. He received a hard stare and no thanks and limped away wishing he hadn't bothered.

He turned his head as one of the children squealed. She was standing in the middle of the rabbit pen and Stuart, the seagull, had dived at her and was busy trying to untie her shoelaces, convinced that they were worms.

"You've no business to have such dangerous creatures here," a woman said, glaring at Martin as if he were to blame.

"Stuart isn't dangerous. He's funny." Martin hobbled into the enclosure and stood beside the little girl. "Look. He thinks you're wearing worms."

She giggled.

"Give him this. He's friendly and very nice when you get to know him, but he simply can't resist anything long and thin. Nor could you if you were

90

a bird."

Bread was infinitely preferable to strips of material that tasted of nothing. Stuart soon forgot his desire, and wandered off towards another child, who was now also holding out a piece of bread.

"I'm not sure I like so many people here at once," Anna Wyn said. "Some children have very hard hands and others deliberately try to hurt the animals. Oh, no!"

One of the boys from the coach party had bent to pick up the Pirate, grabbing him round the middle. He hated being picked up and was only too likely to scratch and scratch hard.

"No," Anna Wyn shouted, and ran across to intervene. But Dannie, who seemed to have eyes that saw everything, was before her, taking the Pirate gently away from the child, and soothing the outraged little animal with a stroking hand. He noticed an irate woman bearing down on them. The woman who had called Stuart dangerous.

The little girl was with her. Brother and sister and neither of them had ever been taught how to approach an animal. Martin took the small boy's hand, and, before his mother could approach him, hobbled off as fast as he was able, towards the pig pen.

"Come and see Susie and Hannah," he said. "Talk to them. Like this."

He grunted.

The two young pigs, enchanted, grunted back at him, and in no time at all three of them were carrying on what appeared to be the most serious conversation. Within minutes, the small boy had joined in too, his eyes alight with laughter.

"You have to understand animals," Martin said, surprising himself. "They get frightened, just like you and me. The kitten thought he was being attacked by an enormous giant. Just lie down on the grass."

The boy stared at him.

"I want to show you something. I won't hurt you."

The boy lay down.

"Now look up at me. How big do I look?"

"Enormous."

Martin, helped the child up and put an arm round his shoulder, kneeling down to do so.

"Now I don't look so big, do I?" he asked. "That's how you looked to the kitten. He didn't know you only wanted to cuddle him. Would you like to come and cuddle one of the rabbits?"

The small boy looked up at Martin, sure he was at least twenty years old. He wasn't used to grown-ups who took him seriously and didn't spend all their time scolding him for doing wrong. Martin knew exactly how he felt.

The rabbit pen was deserted. Martin opened the gate and led the child inside. He knelt on the ground. "Now kneel beside me. Don't move. Pretend you're a garden gnome." The little boy grinned.

Within minutes the rabbits had relaxed and were

playing together again. A white angora nibbled at a lettuce leaf and an enchanting small black rabbit peeped out of a drainpipe put in to simulate a burrow. Anna Wyn had soon learned that rabbits dig and the perimeter had to be concreted. Even so, they sometimes popped up in very unexpected places and each night there was an inspection to see that no new hole had been started.

Martin leaned forward and lifted the little black rabbit, holding it with gentle hands.

"Take him, with one hand under his chest and the other under his tail," he said. "Very gently. Now stroke him. Isn't he soft?"

"He's being good," the boy said. "He isn't wriggling at all."

"That's because you're being gentle and not hurting him. They only wriggle if your hands clutch too hard. You'd wriggle if I picked you up and swung you in the air and my hands bruised you, wouldn't you?"

"Robin," said an angry voice from just behind them. "How many times do I have to tell you not to speak to strange men?"

"I work here," Martin said, anger lending an edge to his voice. He stood up, thankful that the child's mother was smaller than he, and hoping that he looked far older than his almost fifteen years. "Our job is to educate the children. I hardly think I rank as a strange man."

"You don't look like a teacher. They don't dress in jeans. You look thoroughly scruffy."

"You try working with animals in your Sunday best," Martin said, incensed. He felt sorry for the children of such a mother, and wondered why she had come on the coach in the first place.

"Nobody told us we were going to call in at such an insanitary place," the woman said. "We are on a mystery tour. I had expected we would visit places of culture, such as Chatsworth, not a dump like this. Come along, children, we'll sit in the coach and wait for the others to come."

She stalked off, sour-faced.

"Can I stroke the rabbit?" the little girl asked. "Has he a name?"

"Yes. This is Benjy. He used to belong to a little girl like you, but she grew tired of him."

"I wouldn't. Mummy won't let us have rabbits. Nor a cat. Nor a hamster . . . "

"Robin! Susan! Come here at once."

Martin, standing at the counter, where Anna Wyn was making cups of tea by the score, sighed. "There's always one like that in any big group," he said. "Their poor children suffer."

"They'll either grow up as horrible as their mother, or marry and have eight kids and fill the house with pets," Anna Wyn said.

Martin was busy doing sums. Twenty cups of tea at 25p each. Ten cups of coffee at 30p each. Six tins of cola, at 35p each. Children had been buying bars of chocolate, all of them priced differently. His ankle ached and his head was beginning to spin. The energy that had given him courage to stand up to the irate mother was fading, and he felt drained.

He longed to go in and sit down, but there was work to do still.

The coach was in the yard. There was a sudden bark, and as Martin whistled, his reaction automatic, Blue raced towards him. The childrens' mother was standing on the coach step, screaming.

Martin, sure someone had been bitten, hobbled over to her as fast as he could, gritting his teeth as the pain in his ankle flared again.

He expected to find both children covered in blood, but they were sitting quietly in the coach.

"That dog . . . " she was almost speechless with fright.

"What did he do?"

"He walked across and barked. Nobody ought to keep a dog like that. They are very dangerous indeed."

"How did he get out? He was in his run."

"My little boy wanted to see the chickens. He went to look at them, and opened the gate of the dog's pen, thinking that they were in there. The dog wasn't visible. He chased Robin back to the coach."

"He wasn't chasing your son. He wanted to find me," Martin said. "He knew he ought not to be out and didn't know where to go. The farmyard is private," he continued. "It's not part of the park at all. There is a notice on the gate saying 'No admission for unauthorized persons beyond this point.' Surely the child is old enough to read. Anyway, the dog isn't dangerous. He is put in his pen so that children can't annoy or tease him."

"You'll be hearing more about this," the woman said. Her eyes were dark with fury. Martin, looking at her, was glad she was not his mother.

The coach driver looked at Martin and rolled his eyes. The bearded man came over to them, and to their surprise, spoke sharply to the mother.

"The dog did no harm. Your child had no business opening any gate anywhere, either inside the park or outside it. I did ask parents to keep the children under control. I think that the owners of the farm and park have more to complain about than you, Madam. Now please will you take your seat."

Martin walked Blue back to his pen and closed the gate. He oc, ould have done without so much walking. He leaned against the farmyard wall, wishing it was time to close. At least the coach party were moving on. As they began to climb into the coach he dragged himself back to the little shop, where Dannie and Anna Wyn were standing together, dismayed. They still had to rescue Skippy.

They looked at the bearded man, who had come back into the shop, expecting to be told that there would be complaints. Unexpectedly he smiled at them.

"I'm sorry I was so brusque when we came," he said. "Now perhaps you understand why. That woman has been a pain throughout the tour. Most of us are ready to strangle her. I hope this will make up for what must have been a very tiresome afternoon."

He handed them two £10 notes and walked off.

"How wrong can you be?" Dannie said. "This calls for a celebration," he added. "As soon as the last customer has gone I'll treat you both to a bar of chocolate!"

Anna Wyn laughed.

"And then we have to begin Operation Skippy," she said. "After that, we'll need another celebration."

"More likely to need arnica for the bruises. And a good bath," Dannie said. "Anyway, his rescue can't possibly be as traumatic as the rest of the afternoon."

Afterwards Martin wondered if someone had been listening and was determined to prove Dannie wrong.

Chapter 11

Skippy, provided with a pile of hay, seemed happy on his mound. His big ears flickered in response to Anna Wyn's voice, but he was determined to make the most of this extra bonus. He switched his tail as he fed.

Martin sat on the wall.

"There's no way we can haul him out of that," he said. "He's far to heavy for the three of us to lift."

"He'd smash us to pieces with his hooves." Anna Wyn had had enough of the day. "Do you think that woman will make trouble?"

Dannie, who was considering the situation, frowned.

"I don't see why she should. The Tour Leader, or whatever they call him, seemed to have her under control. He would never have given us an extra twenty pounds if he agreed with her."

"I sometimes wish we'd never started to open to the public," Anna Wyn said.

"And how would you make the money to feed the animals and birds? You'd have to get rid of them. You are doing good work. Don't let it get you down. Bound to have some difficult people at times. Most enjoy it. They say so, don't they, in the visitors' book?"

"We've made well over a hundred pounds this afternoon, " Martin said. "Seventy-four from the coach trip. Which is twenty more than we would have had if that woman hadn't cut up rough."

"And they've cleared us out of chocolate bars, crisps and cola," Dannie said.

Martin grinned suddenly. "One small girl had so much money to spend she bought four ice creams and three bars of chocolate and ate them all. Then she was sick."

"Serve her right." Anna Wyn sighed." That means an extra shopping trip to the cash and carry." She was determined to see the worst side of everything.

"Operation Skippy," Dannie said. "Come on. He can't stay there all night."

"We'll be here half the night as it is. All the animals have to be fed and shut away, and it's after five now."

Martin had a sudden desire to shake his stepsister. Dannie noticed his expression and intervened.

"Martin, go and get a pile of sandwiches for us.

Anna Wyn, start your feeding round. I want to think. I've half an idea, but Skippy might not go along with it."

Martin had several ideas too. His trip to the farmhouse kitchen would give him more time to work them out.

Leah always made sure that there were packs of sandwiches, neatly wrapped, in the refrigerator, as well as in the deep freeze, as insurance against emergencies, which seemed to happen all the time. Martin took three packs, then rummaged until he found several small cartons of fruit juice.

His ankle hurt, but he felt almost elated as he walked back to the Sanctuary, his mind on the afternoon's visit. It had gone so well, and maybe the Tour Operator would recommend them to other coach owners. This week there would be more than enough money to cover the cost of feed and some over. Money to bank.

For the first time he saw a gleam in the dark. They would make the Sanctuary pay. Anna Wyn would realize that when she was less tired.

He returned to find Dannie struggling with an old door that he'd found in one of the farm buildings.

Martin put the sandwich packs down on a table near the shop, and took one end of the door. "It ought to stretch from the mound to the wall. Though I'm not sure how Skippy will feel about walking the plank. It's not going to be the steadiest of bridges."

"It'll have a slope on it," Martin said. "The top of the mound is higher than the wall."

Anna Wyn's yell alerted them.

"Eddy's jumped out. He's after the sandwiches." She was struggling with two full buckets of water.

The little white goat was also struggling as he tried to pull the wrapping off one of the sandwich packs.

"These buckets weigh more every day. I think they've filled our tanks with heavy water." Anna Wyn put them down and cursed as water slopped over her shoes.

Martin lifted the little goat. He was still small enough to carry, though that wouldn't last much longer.

"Another two planks on that fence tomorrow." Martin looked at the goats' enclosure. There were already six extra rails, intended to keep Eddy within bounds. The last one had been added at the end of the previous week and everyone had been sure that neither of the kids would be able to jump it.

Eddy, held firmly under the chest and behind his tail, decided it was wiser not to struggle. He knew that humans were stronger than he was, and his escapes always ended in capture and return. Also, if he came quietly, he was rewarded.

Martin grabbed a carrot on his way past the full bucket that was waiting for distribution, pushed it into Eddy's mouth and shut him in Skippy's shed, which was nearer than the goat run. Tammy, his sister, was bleating noisily.

"I thought that barrier was Eddy-proof," Anna Wyn said. She leaned against an aviary cage. The two striped and lively chipmunks who had replaced several birds that had been released to fly free, perched behind her, looking interested. It was time for food.

The Pirate thought so too. He climbed the wire and sat hopefully on top of the cage, fishing through it with a busy paw. Chipmunks might taste good. The two little animals were dashing round their cage, terrified. Martin, remembering Taid's saying that it never rained but it poured, grabbed the cat, smacked him, and shut him an empty cage, where he moaned loudly at his loss of freedom. Spider and Ginger, his mother, investigating the frantic cries, were also put inside.

"They'd only come and help. Skippy doesn't like cats," Anna Wyn said. She sighed. "If I don't eat I'll fall over."

"Kettle should've boiled," Dannie said. "I plugged it in on my way to the barn. Let's make a banquet of it and have coffee."

"We ought to be feeding the animals. And freeing Skippy."

"Can't if we all die of starvation and exhaustion," Dannie yawned. "It's been a long day. He's not suffering and it won't hurt any of them to wait twenty minutes."

Martin glanced at his watch. He ought to be

feeding Blue, and changing the bedding in Caley's stable, which he hadn't had time to do before. Lola needed her food too. No use complaining. Anna Wyn had hours of work ahead of her, as the afternoon had been so busy that she had not had a chance to do any of the odd jobs that were often fitted in when they had few visitors.

Dannie filled the three mugs. He put one pound in the cash box and produced three chocolate bars from his pocket.

"Pinched them before the horde cleaned us out," he said. "Didn't have time to pay."

"You could have had them free." Anna Wyn smiled suddenly. "You know, I've only just realized that was a terrific afternoon. We've made enough to stand ourselves two more chocolate bars each." They were suddenly light-hearted, in spite of Skippy's mishap.

Anna Wyn yawned and stretched. "Am I whacked!" She bit into a cheese and tomato sandwich. "Martin, if there's one thing your mother does well, it's cook. You've no idea what life was like before she came. Burned baked beans on toast nearly every day, and muesli in between."

"Don't you mean baked beans and burned toast?" Dannie asked.

"No. We have a toaster. We put the baked beans in a pan on the Aga and as often as not forgot them. I'd forgive anyone anything if they cooked like Leah."

She laughed.

"Da's speciality was thick bread doorsteps and cheese and pickles. Taid is a wizard at eggs and bacon and fried bread but that gets tiresome too if you have it at every meal."

Martin looked, at her, startled. He had always taken his mother's cooking for granted and had never realized that she was exceptional.

Dannie grinned.

"What do you think made me want to stay on here?" he asked. "I came into a kitchen that smelled of delights. Not smelled anything like it since I stayed with my Great Aunt Petula who made the most delicious stews."

"Nobody could have a great Aunt called Petula," Anna Wyn laughed. "I can tackle anything now. I always feel grouchy when I'm hungry. Let's find out if Skippy will walk the plank."

Skippy was restive. The hay had all gone and his prison allowed very little movement.

Martin and Dannie manoeuvred the door into place, with the greatest difficulty, as there proved to be very few flat places on the mound.

After almost fifteen minutes of useless struggle, Dannie fetched a spade and dug out a flat recess which just fitted round the door and anchored it securely. It balanced across the top of the wall, which was made of brick and several inches wide.

Anna Wyn, standing on the door, holding out a carrot, called to the little donkey. He adored carrots, but he was not at all sure that he wanted to trust himself to so strange a contraption. He brayed.

Maggie, hungry and cross because of it, answered him from her enclosure. Caley, tethered by the pig pen, kicked his empty bucket, which made a very satisfying noise.

The five Chinese geese left their grandstand view of the Guinea pig enclosure and went to see what Caley was doing. Caley stamped at them. He didn't like the geese. "It's a good job we have no neighbours," Anna Wyn said. "The noise level here must be well above the permitted range. Oh, come on Skippy. Don't be so daft. It's quite safe. I'm on it, aren't I?"

Skippy put his two front hooves on the door. They clattered, and he bucked and retreated.

"Good job I anchored that end thoroughly," Dannie said. "OK, Annie Winnie?"

"Call me that and you won't be OK." Anna Wyn moved across the door and held the carrot almost under Skippy's nose. As he reached for it, she retreated. He followed her, until again his hooves clattered on the wood.

This time he jumped sideways and slid, almost into the ditch. Anna Wyn hauled him up by his mane. He rubbed his grey head against her, but his eyes told her that there was no way at all that he intended to cross that particular obstacle.

"We could dig a path out and break down the wall for him, I suppose," Dannie said, by now almost as glum as Anna Wyn. "That's right,

Martin, leave us to it," he added, as Martin turned and walked away towards the gate of the animal park.

He returned, dragging a wide plank.

"There's another one. If we can make sides to the bridge, so that he can't see down, he might come."

Dannie went for the little tractor and trailer, and drove it back filled with all kinds of pieces of wood. By the time they had finished the whole contraption looked like something dreamed up by a cartoonist, but so long as Skippy didn't touch the sides, that were only propped in place, all would be well.

He stared at them, and looked hopefully at the carrot, as Anna Wyn held it out again.

Martin went into the shop. He found a number of carrots waiting to be fed to the ponies, and sliced them into pieces. He returned to find that Skippy was standing, looking thoughtful, at the entrance to his escape route.

Martin laid the carrot pieces on the ground, just out of reach, in a trail that led to safety.

Half-way across, eating as he went, the little donkey lifted his head. He saw space, and grass on which he could run, and freedom.

As he charged across the makeshift sides collapsed, but he was on his own ground. Martin led him to his enclosure and he spent the next few minutes racing and bucking, restored to long forgotten baby days by his adventure.

106

"I don't think I'll be able to walk again for days," Martin said, as he carried Eddy back to his own enclosure and shut him in with his sister, leaving the two of them to dip deep into their feed tubs.

"Thank goodness we've Taid to do the hand-feeding," Anna Wyn said, as at last they shut the gate of the park behind them, and went through into the farmyard.

When they went into the kitchen they were met with anxious faces.

"Taid had a fall," Leah said. "Gwyn's gone with him to the hospital. They think he's broken his thigh."

Chapter 12

Martin felt as if the next two weeks passed in a daze. Everyone was worried about Taid. Nobody had realized how much work he actually did. Martin missed him more than he had thought possible. The old man was always ready to listen, to advise, and to offer suggestions.

It was Taid who came to calm Caley when he was in a passion. It was Taid who helped with Blue, and who fed the dogs. It was Taid who sat and hand fed sick animals. Taid who smooothed bad tempers. Taid who kept the family from each other's throats.

Tempers flared, and everyone seemed to be racing against time. Leah visited the hospital in the afternoon, Gwyn in the evening. Martin twice took a bus into Bangor. The first time he went the hospital ward unnerved him and Taid looked so forlorn, his face grey with pain, his eyes almost vacant. He had little energy and Martin left after quarter of an hour, and returned home depressed and miserable.

But by the second visit, ten days later, Taid was almost himself again, and teased Martin when he took grapes, not knowing what else to bring the old man.

"Soon be back plaguing you all," he said, and grinned at his step-grandson. "It will be nice to taste Leah's cooking again; nobody could say much about the food here. Feeds you, is all, and sometimes it doesn't do that. Ask Gwyn to bring me in a nice ham sandwich."

Martin laughed and promised to deliver the message. He went home far happier and found Anna Wyn sitting, exhausted, in Taid's big chair.

"I hope nobody brings in any more injured animals," she said. "I just cant cope."

"Asked for it, didn't you," Dannie commented, with a sigh, as there was a knock on the door. It was a telephone engineer, carrying a cardboard box.

"Found it on the road," the man said. "Knew you'd do something for the poor creature."

He went, and left the three of them looking at the box as if it might bite them.

The fox cub swore as Anna Wyn lifted the lid. She stared at it helplessly. At the gaping wound on its shoulder, and the hind leg that lay at such an odd angle.

Martin had never seen a fox so close before. Sharp nosed, prick eared, and malevolent, it glared at him from eyes that were wild with fear and pain.

"It would be an added attraction if we got it fit," Dannie said.

"How much would the vet charge for setting that leg and healing that wound? And what do we feed it on?"

"Dog food," Dannie said. "Not half as much a problem as the heron."

"Luckily the Sea Zoo is helping us out with fish," Anna Wyn said. "They're giving us a special price for his supply, which is just as well as he has the most tremendous appetite."

"When will he be well enough to release?" Dannie put a hand towards the fox and withdrew it hastily, just seconds away from the snapped teeth.

"The fox? Probably never, with that leg. He won't be able to walk properly; it might even have to be amputated."

"I meant the heron."

"In a couple of weeks, hopefully. He's trying to fly again. The broken wing has healed well, but it isn't strong enough yet."

Anna Wyn hurriedly put the lid on the box as her father approached. He stared at them as if looking through them.

"Da? What is it?"

Gwyn seated himself on the window seat, pushing Spider out of his way, and ran his hands through his hair. "Taid," he said, running his fingers through his hair. "He had a heart attack. He's dead. The hospital have just phoned. He was doing so well and looking forward to coming home next week."

No one could believe it. They had seen him only yesterday, laughing, talking, grumbling about the horrid little pork pie and apology for a salad that had been given him for lunch that day.

"He was eighty-four," Gwyn said. "You'd never have thought it . . . "

It was impossible to believe that Taid was gone. That he would never walk into the kitchen again. Never tease Martin again. Never help with the farm again.

Martin wanted to be alone, to come to terms with the idea. To grieve in his own way for the one person in the family who had always had time for him, and had done so much for Blue.

Dannie put an arm round Anna Wyn, who looked as if the world had ended.

A car drove into the yard, and three excited children raced into the shop. Gwyn stood up, and looked at Dannie.

"We can't just shut. There's so much to do."

He walked heavily away, and for the first time Martin felt a pang of sympathy for his stepfather, and wanted to go to him and say how much he minded about losing Taid. But the words wouldn't come and the moment passed.

"The show goes on," Dannie said, an hour later, bringing out three mugs of black coffee. He looked at Anna Wyn. "Tears have to wait, love. What do we do about this fox?"

"I can sell Lola's piglets," Martin said. "I don't know how much they're worth, though . . . or if it will be enough."

A tall man, who had followed the children, was looking with interest at Dannie's shelf, which was filled with his wooden animals.

"I like these," he said. "I want to buy one for each of the children . . . to remember a red letter day."

"What kind of red letter day?" Dannie asked. Anna Wyn was finding it difficult to speak at all.

"I've been out of work for some months. I started a new job four weeks ago, and I promised that as soon as I got my first pay cheque we'd celebrate. My wife couldn't come. She's gone back to nursing and she had to work."

He was bubbling over with happiness, sure everyone must share his feelings. He turned over the little wooden beasts, and finally chose a seal, a mountain goat and a bucking pony. Martin, leading each child round the sanctuary, as they all wanted pony rides, couldn't get Taid out of his mind.

Taid would have loved to see the fox. Taid would never be there to see the Noah's Ark . . . if it were ever built.

There were questions to answer. Martin gave ten rides that day. He made double journeys, and charged double. He regretted his rashness in extending the distance, as his ankle ached long before they were over. He did not intend to give up. He limped on, longing for closing time.

At last it was five o'clock on the longest day of his life. All the animals and birds were fed, and locked away for the night. As they went into the yard, Martin realized that everywhere there were memories of the old man. His front door was closed. It always stood open in the summer. On fine days he sat in the doorway, happy to talk to the visitors, who found him full of information.

Gwyn came out of the kennel where Taid's two dogs lay, forlorn, noses on their paws.

"They know, poor beasts," Gwyn said.

"How do they know?"

"From us, from our mood, I suppose. I don't know how else. A dog can sense death in a house. Or death of a dog it's known well." He sighed.

"If only I'd realized he was feeling his age . . . we never thought. He ought not to have been working."

"Can you imagine Taid sitting down and doing nothing?" Leah asked. "Come and eat. We'll all feel better for a meal."

Martin went into the kitchen, feeling virtuous. All his animals were fed. Caley, unsaddled and groomed, was in his stable, bedded on clean straw, tugging at his haynet.

"I did it for you, Taid," he said inside his head, wondering if perhaps the old man could hear him, from some place unimaginable. How could life just vanish, as if a candle flame had been put out?

113

Dilys, coming into the kitchen, stared at them.

"What's up with you all? It's like a morgue in here."

Anna Wyn put down her cup and ran out of the room.

"Taid's dead, love," Leah said. "He had a heart attack. They said it was very quick; no time for him to feel any pain. In his sleep."

Dilys stood, staring at them, sudden tears flooding down her face.

"I didn't know. . . I didn't mean . . . oh, damn it . . . I wouldn't have said . . . "

"How could you know?" Gwyn asked. "It doesn't matter . . . I mean, what you said doesn't matter." Taid's jacket hung on the door. Gwyn walked over and took it down, smoothing the folds, stroking the material, and then walked off with it, to put it back in the cottage next door. He whistled to Taid's two dogs and took them into the cottage with him. The front door slammed shut.

Leah went out of the room. Dilys sat down, and looked at them, her eyes miserable. "I wish I'd known. Why didn't they ring me?"

"Your dad was knocked for six and the rest of us have been worked off our feet," Dannie said. "Visitors all day and all of them wanted sandwiches. Leah hadn't a minute . . . nor had we . . . and I don't suppose Gwyn thought. He had enough to do, too. You know what it's like. Not as if he could leave the animals without food or water, or cleaning out."

Even Dannie was subdued.

Martin decided to visit Mervyn next day and find out how much he could expect if he sold his piglets to someone who would take them on and fatten them for market. It would save him money on feed.

Dilys went upstairs to comfort her sister.

"You can't give all the money for your carvings to the Sanctuary," Martin said to Dannie. "It isn't fair."

"I would if I lived here, and was part of the farm, so why not?" Dannie asked.

"You're not."

"I've plans," Dannie said. "Can you keep a secret?"

My life's full of secrets I never share, Martin thought, but didn't say it aloud. He nodded.

"How would you like me as a stepbrother-in-law?"

Martin stared at him.

"Dilys?"

"No. Anna Wyn, if I can ever get her mind off her animals. Maybe I'd better break a leg. That would rouse her interest!"

He laughed, and then remembered.

"Taid knew what was in my mind," he said. "No one else has guessed. Not even Anna Wyn. It'll take time, but there's plenty of that. She's young, but that'll change and I can wait."

Martin walked across to the window, limping.

"Ankle sore?"

He nodded. It had been a very tough day.

He thought miserably of all the things he had never said to Taid, and now never would. Better to think of the future. "It'd be great if you did marry Anna Wyn."

"Keep it dark. I'd hate you to tell her I was going to propose before I get the chance."

There were footsteps on the stairs. Martin made a sign with his hand, across his heart, and across his throat. Cross my heart and hope to die, if I ever tell. Dannie put his thumb up as the door opened and Leah came in. She sat on the window seat, staring into the distance.

"I hadn't realized how much we'd miss him," she said. "Mervyn will miss him too. They enjoyed meeting and talking over old times."

Martin suddenly realized he would have to tell Tag. The little boy had adored Taid and spent hours with him, missing his own grandparents. The American family were off to the States for a holiday, and to visit friends and family, in a couple of days' time. Ought he to tell them now, or wait until they came back? He didn't know.

Gwyn appeared in the doorway, the two dogs behind him. They came in to the kitchen, behaving as if afraid that someone might shout at them to get out. Blue went across and sniffed both of them, making sure he knew them. Satisfied, he returned to his corner. The two collies walked across and cuddled up against him, as if asking for sympathy.

Martin, looking at them, felt a sudden lump in

his throat and an ache inside him. He had never before realized that Taid was special, and always had a kind word when everyone else was cross with him. It was only now that he knew that the most important person, to him, in his little world, had been taken away from him for ever. How would they ever manage without the old man?

Chapter 13

The churchyard was bright with flowers, and heavy with grief. The family stood together. Martin, looking around, was surprised at the number of village people who had come to say goodbye to Taid.

Martin felt stiff and awkward, and did not know what to say to anyone. He felt more of an alien than ever, especially as nobody seemed to be speaking English.

"Elwyn will be at home here. So many of his friends went before him," Megan the Lump said. It was some moments before Martin realized that Taid was Elwyn. He had never before heard anyone use the old man's Christian name. To all the family and even to Dai and Dannie, the milkman and the postman, he was always Taid.

There were so many people here, and so many who he didn't even know.

He was still an alien, a loner, and would be more alone than ever now Taid had gone. Nobody had time for him. Even Dannie seemed to have eyes for no one but Anna Wyn.

Martin wished he could have brought Blue with him. The dog was company and re-assurance.

Taid had been a friend, but he had never realized it. Now the old man was only a ghost whisper on the wind, a memory, and a sudden terrible ache as Martin watched the coffin brought out, and heard the minister speaking the last words over the open grave.

He did not understand the Welsh but the sound was musical. He stood, isolated, watching, longing to be part of the group that seemed to have forgotten him.

Leah stood beside Gwyn, who had a word for everyone, and many to thank for the flowers they sent. Gwyn was unfamiliar in a black suit that must have come out of the wardrobe for other funeral occasions. Martin had never seen if before.

His mother was wearing a dark grey coat that he recognized from the time before her marriage. It was out of fashion, and Leah never wore it any more. She spent much of her life as they all did, in jeans and wellingtons and anorak.

Taid had been a good man and he was spoken of with affection. There were flowers to remember him, heaps of scarlet, purple and gold, shining green leaves and tawny sprays. A crook made of flowers held pride of place. The bright blooms were piled high on the coffin and later, beside the grave.

The church steeple was stark against mountains that today were clear to view. Birds were singing. The skies should have been grey, rain pouring from heavy clouds, not an uncaring sun that shone brilliantly on all of them. "A grand day . . . grass growing weather." Taid's voice was an echo in his ears.

Martin watched the coffin lowered into the grave, and thought of the old man as he had been a year before, out on the hills with Blue, teaching Martin how to teach his dog. He had never thanked his tutor; had never realized he needed to thank him and now it was impossible.

Martin had picked flowers from Taid's garden. Sadly, he laid them beside the wreaths that covered the ground. Taid would never smell roses again, never pick himself a buttonhole, revelling in the colour and shape.

Later, the farmhouse was full of people. Leah and the two girls had been busy from early morning, preparing a buffet. The visitors stood in little groups, remembering. The Animal Park was closed for the day.

Martin needed to be alone. The noise and busy voices seemed all wrong. There should be silence, and time to remember.

He whistled to Blue and walked into the sanctuary field.

He felt drained of energy, and empty of all emotion.

There were weeds growing in the flowerbeds. He sat on his haunches and pulled them out, one by one, each a tribute, that fulfilled a need. He loathed weeding, and had done it under duress, with Taid making him work.

Today it satisfied him in a way he had never known before.

Taid had loved the brown earth, the growing buds, the promise of future bounty. The sight of the weedfree earth, when he had finished, gave Martin a thrill of pleasure, as if the old man's thoughts had taken over part of his brain.

It was the first time he understood how much Taid had enjoyed his days among the flowers.

Whatever happened, the birds and animals had to be fed. He was halfway through the chores when Dannie joined him. They worked side by side, in silence, neither feeling like words. Martin's ankle nagged him, but he felt the pain a small penance beside the loss of the man who, he realized, had been his greatest friend.

Martin stayed in the sanctuary until the sun went down and the mountains were hidden by darkness. Blue lay in the shop doorway and watched, used to the routine, seeming to understand his master's need.

He looked round the enclosures. All the animals

were in for the night, the doors of their houses padlocked. Anna Wyn had insisted on padlocks since the day that Skippy had been let out to fall into the Guinea pig enclosure.

The place was strangely silent. He went to feed Caley. Dannie had already bedded the pony on clean straw. Maggie and Sukie and the donkey slept outside during the summer, unless there was a thunderstorm. Anna Wyn was afraid a tree might be struck by lightning, with the ponies sheltering beneath it. Maggie was afraid of lightning, and apt to panic.

The kitchen was deserted, though the remains of the buffet was still on the table. Martin found a large plate. He collected sandwiches and sausage rolls and slices of quiche and walnut cake to take upstairs.

He had a feeling that he ought not to want to eat at all, that it was disloyal to Taid's memory, but his work had made him extra hungry.

He sat on the window seat in his room, with Blue beside him. The farmyard seemed more empty than usual, which was absurd, as Taid rarely came out of his cottage in the evenings. Yet Martin expected the door to open and the old man to appear and walk towards the house, calling his dogs as he came.

It was so hard to realize that would never happen again.

Martin was thirsty. He had forgotten to bring up anything to drink, but he could not face the kitchen again, or meeting any of the family. None of them seemed able to find any words to say to each other, other than those that were absolutely necessary.

There was a tentative tap on the door. Martin stared, as if able to see through it. Nobody ever knocked on his door. Fearing some stranger stood there, bringing more bad news, he opened it and was amazed to see his stepfather, looking more familiar now he was back in his working clothes.

"Can I come in?"

"Sure," Martin said, but felt a little stab of fear. What had he done wrong now?

Gwyn held a long package in his hand. He set it on the desk he had bought for Martin so that he could do his homework in peace. He sat in the chair by the bed.

"It feels all wrong, without Taid," he said. "Felt wrong working today, the day he was buried, but animals need feeding, no matter what."

He sighed. He appeared to have forgotten why he had come. Gwyn's face was grey and his eyes were haunted.

"Taid was making you something special for your birthday. He won't ever finish it now, but maybe Dannie will help you to do so. I thought you might like it now. For his grandson, he said, when I asked him who he intended it for. He'd always wanted a lad to teach about the dogs."

Martin sat speechless.

"I wanted a son too," Gwyn said.

There was a long pause before he spoke again.

"Those two dogs of Taid's . . . they lift their heads at every footstep . . . every time the door opens . . . and then sink back again into misery because it's never the right person. I don't know if I can bear it . . . but I can't put them down."

"Will they get over it?" Martin asked.

"Given time, most dogs do."

Martin looked at the oddly shaped parcel, wondering what was inside.

"Open it," Gwyn said.

He removed the brown paper. A lump rose in his throat and tears stang behind his eyes. He swallowed, and walked across to the window, and stood with his back to his stepfather, staring out at the cobbled yard, latched with light from the house windows.

Taid had carved him a crook; the doghead handle was Blue, his ears pricked, his mouth slightly open, the tongue just showing. He held it in his hand, knowing that it was one of the last things that Taid had touched. Taid had always made crooks, beautiful things with carved handles. They were often given as prizes at the local Sheepdog Trials. Martin had longed for one.

"When you've learned to train a dog," Taid said. "When I make you one, you'll know you've passed my tests."

The wood was rough, as yet unpolished. The old man hadn't had time to finish it. That could easily be remedied. The carving was perfect.

He couldn't say anything. After a few minutes he felt his stepfather's hand grip his shoulder.

The door closed. For the first time Martin felt a liking for his stepfather and was halfway to understanding him.

That night, when he went to bed, the crook lay beside him and he held on to the handle as if it might bring Taid back.

Outside in the dark owls cried and fox cubs barked, and Skippy, for some reason known only to himself, brayed at the moon, as if mourning for a lost companion, startling every creature for miles around.

Chapter 14

It became a relief when Gwyn took the dogs across to Taid's cottage. They lay by day either by the cottage door, or in the kitchen, ears pricked at every footstep, a look of hope on the two wise faces.

It was never the person they needed.

Noses dropped on paws, they watched, unmoving, until the next time someone alerted them by coming into the yard. Only Blue could reach them. He lay beside them. He followed them. He waited until they had fed, although neither seemed to have much appetite.

Nobody seemed to have time for Martin. He worked by day among the animals. He found the notice Taid had been painting and finished it.

It read "Bryn Gwynt Animal Park and Wildlife Sanctuary."

It was written in both Welsh and English.

They would need other notices along the road to attract passing motorists.

Taid had been dead for two weeks. Gwyn still vanished every evening.

"What does he do in there?" He asked his mother at the beginning of the third week after the old man's death.

Leah dropped wearily into a chair, hugging a mug of tea. She pushed the plate of scones across to Martin.

"There's so much to do," she said. "All Taid's clothes to be sorted and packed for the Oxfam shop. His papers to go through. His pension book to go back. We had so many letters of sympathy and so many people sent flowers. We have to write to them all and thank them. It's more peaceful there than here. He can sit at Taid's desk and get on with it without interruption."

She sipped her tea, and took a scone, but instead of eating it, crumbled it on to the plate, as if she had no idea that she was doing so.

"There will be a valuer here soon to work out the death duties, I suppose," she said. "I don't understand how the farm worked, and your father won't talk to me. He sits there, night after night, and I worry."

"Death duties? Doesn't the farm belong to Gwyn?" Martin was so startled that he'd shouted at his mother.

"I don't even know that, son." Leah pushed her

hair away from her face. "Taid gave Gwyn the farmhouse when he married. I do know that. Taid kept the cottage and, so far as I know, he owned the farm. He didn't want to part with that. I never thought of the muddle it might cause when he did die. It's something you dont really anticipate."

Martin, always aware of finance, stared at his mother.

"What sort of death duty?"

"I'm not sure of the exact figures. They change so often at budget time. I think it's forty percent of anything over somewhere in the region of a hundred and twenty thousand pounds. Farms are worth more than that, with the buildings and stock and machinery. Gwyn knows farmers who have had to sell their stock to pay the death duties."

She frowned down at her hands, which were twisting the edge of her jersey. "If Gwyn has to sell up . . . can you imagine him away from the farm?"

She offered a scone to Blue, who thought that Heaven had come early and gobbled it fast lest she change her mind.

"I lie awake, having nightmares about it. My only hope is that farms aren't like ordinary property, but I don't know. The girls don't know either, and I can't worry them."

"We couldd be bankrupt," Martin said, his mind full of columns that never seemed to add up to anything like a profit. "What would we all do?" There was always news of farms that had to sell up. That had seemed remote, nothing to do with them.

"I don't know. I don't think that Taid had made any provisions. He never made a will. He hated the thought. He made Gwyn angry as he took his share of the money and never put any of it into the farm or the machinery. We don't even know what he did with it. He never consulted a solicitor. Your father is going through his papers, trying to find out just what has happened to his half of any profit."

"Didn't Gwyn ask?"

"Often. It was the one thing that made Taid angry. 'Can't wait for me to die,' he kept shouting, the only time it was mentioned in my hearing. I think they had other rows, but never in front of me."

She stroked Blue's ears. He, always sensitive to peoples' feelings, leaned against her knee and looked at her anxiously, as if afraid that he had unknowingly transgressed and was the cause of the odd feelings in the room.

Only another week and Martin would be back at school. Another year before he could leave. His mother wanted him to stay on, but Martin knew he was needed. If they kept the farm. A black abyss formed in his mind.

Gwyn, without the farm, would be desolate. He was born to it, bred to it. He was out of bed at five every morning, racing downstairs, eager to start the day, to discover what had happened overnight, what had grown, what been born.

Anna Wyn would not be able to keep her sanctuary if they went elsewhere. It needed land. They had worked so hard and built up so much. Whose was the sanctuary? Was that part of Taid's estate? Had all those birds and animals a value of their own? Maybe Dannie would marry his stepsister soon and they would find somewhere to carry on. Dilys was fine; she had her job.

He felt stifled by worry. Outside in the yard a thin moon lent light. He whistled to Blue and walked into the Animal Park. There were murmurs and faint rustles, but most of the animals were asleep, shut in for the night.

He realized that for the first time his mother had spoken to him as if he were an adult, not a boy who was a nuisance, often making more work than his share. He had thought the adult world would have fewer problems, but he glimpsed some so huge that they were overwhelming.

He realized too that his mother sometimes shared his own loneliness. She knew as little as he about the overall finances of the farm.

Taid had never meant to leave such a mess. He just hadn't wanted to think of a time when he was no longer around.

There was a soft rustle and a sudden wild honking, terror in the noise. Blue leaped, and Martin ran. There was something in the goose pen. A rangy shape turned, a goose held in its jaws. Blue, raging, leaped the fence, and flew in.

The fox dropped the goose. She crept to a far

corner, leaving a trail of dark blood. The other geese were panicking, but the gander, too brave for his own good, ran at the fox, head down, wings flapping, beak open to bite.

Blue was faster.

The intruder snapped at the dog, dodged, and leaped the railings. Blue, about to follow, stopped at Martin's command.

"He left his supper behind," Martin said. "I don't want you hurt. This one's bad enough."

He picked her up, and tucked her under his arm. By the time he reached the kitchen Anna Wyn and Dannie were eating, both silent, as if too exhausted to even think.

They stared at the burden he was carrying. She had a bad tear in her throat and a damaged wing.

Gwyn, coming into the room behind Martin, looked at the goose.

"That one has to go," he said. "There's no way we can go on meeting bills for all these injured creatures of yours, Anna Wyn. Dilys can take Taid's dogs with her tomorrow. They're old and can't earn their keep any more. No more passengers. They'll have to be put to sleep."

He turned and went out again, leaving behind him a silence that was more expressive than a shout.

Chapter 15

The conspiracy started secretly, without any discussion.

Anna Wyn and Dannie dressed the goose's injuries and tucked her into warm straw in one of the sheds. Next morning Martin fed Taid's dogs early, and Dilys took them and the goose in her car.

Anna Wyn went with her. Later she and Dannie returned together, and, passing the kitchen window, Dannie put his thumb up. The goose was in his garden shed, and both dogs safely in his kitchen.

Gwyn, finding them gone, took for granted that Dilys had had them all destroyed.

The last week of the summer holiday was the busiest they had known. Martin, at the till, did constant sums in his head. If only there was money this year to tide them over the winter. The animals didn't stop eating just because the Animal Park had to close. At the moment it was more hospital than park, with too many patients in need of treatment.

They would stay open until the last weekend in October, but business was never brisk after the children went back to school.

There hadn't been time for the Noah's Ark. There hadn't been time for Dannie's assault course or pony trekking. Both Martin and Dannie spilled ideas, but were kept so busy that they remained in their heads. The long winter lay ahead, and they were both eager to start on the projects they had in mind.

If only Gwyn would agree. Now Martin wondered if Gwyn would be able to agree. If they borrowed even £60,000 from the bank, the interest would come to an astronomical sum every month. Never mind paying off the capital.

None of the sheep would fetch a high price; not with the market as it was. Could they sell land?

Martin hadn't even realized that he was thinking as if he belonged. Bryn Gwynt had become home and he couldn't bear to think of losing it. Moreover, he wanted to go on working with animals. Blue had triggered his interest.

Gwyn worked by day on the farm, worked by night in the cottage, and grew grimmer. Leah dared not tell him her fears. They were all walking around like zombies, going through the motions of feeding animals, cleaning pens and sheds and sties and stables, making polite conversation to the summer visitors, who were on holiday and enjoying themselves.

"I feel as if I'm waiting for the sky to fall in," Martin said, at the end of the Monday of their last week before he had to go back to school. They had closed but one small family was still walking round. A tiny girl played happily in the sand pit, setting up a frustrated yell of fury when her parents called her to leave.

Dannie, counting money so that he could write up the day's takings in Anna Wyn's record book, made a sign to be silent.

"There's ways and means," he said, as he wrote down the total. "We are beginning to shape up. We've had more than eight hundred people this week and they were all in holiday mood, so we sold some of my animals as well. This week's takings are the highest we've had; nearly a thousand pounds."

"Two month's winter feed if we're lucky," Anna Wyn said. "How's Rosie, Dannie?"

It was a moment before Martin remembered that Rosie was the injured goose.

"Noisy, hungry, but not at all bad," Dannie said. "The move has done Taid's dogs good. New place; new smells, and they're coming to life. They may be old, but they're still pretty spry. Mott caught a rabbit in my field yesterday. He was astounded.

134

He had no idea what dogs do with rabbits. He let it go again and watched it run off, apparently none the worse."

They laughed at the thought of the old dog, bewildered by his sudden success.

"Blue likes bringing hedgehogs in," Martin said. "I can't imagine why they don't hurt his mouth, but they don't seem to."

"Too late for a cup of tea?" the father of the family asked, putting his head round the shop door. Although it was after five o'clock the sun was still hot.

"Seeing it's you, we'll do it as a favour," Dannie said, laughing. He grinned at the little boy and tugged his hair gently. "And we'll join you."

Martin plugged in the kettle and found chocolate bars for the children and crisps for their parents. The small girl, looking at the shelves, clamoured for one of Dannie's wooden elephants. The money record book would have to be done again, but who cared?

We eat, talk and dream money, Martin thought, but how can anyone help it? Nothing comes free.

The mother was delving in an enormous tapestry bag. She produced a box of cream cakes, and plastic plates and offered them to everyone.

"These are terrific," Dannie said, biting into soft pastry topped with chocolate icing and filled with cream.

"I've a baker's shop," the man said. "I've been thinking. Every week we throw out sacks full of unsold bread and scones and cakes. Could you use them? Might as well bring them here as put them out to go on the tip."

"Bread and scones, yes," Anna Wyn said, her eyes alight with excitement. "Geese, birds, even as treats for the ponies and the donkey. It would be marvellous."

"What about winter, when you're closed?"

"They still eat," Dannie said.

"So do the children." Their mother cut a chocolate bar into two and offered them half each. Her husband grinned at her and took a whole one.

"My daddy is a great big pig," the little girl said, glaring at her father.

"Why?" asked Dannie, half-guessing at the answer.

"We only get half a bar. He always has a whole one." It was hard not to laugh at the disgust in her voice.

"He's bigger than you," Martin said. "Our little ponies don't get nearly as much food as a big horse does. Besides," he added, "just think. If you ate as much as your daddy you'd be as fat as that big pig over there yourself."

Hannah grunted indignantly, and the little girl laughed.

"What does she eat?" her brother asked.

Martin felt amusement bubble inside him. Small children could be fun, for a short while.

"Pignuts," he said.

"What does the pony eat?"

"Ponynuts."

"What do the goats eat?"

"Goatnuts!"

"And birds eat birdnuts, and squirrels eat squirrelnuts and donkeys eat donkeynuts and . . . " Both children were shouting.

"Little girls eat monkeynuts," Dannie said, ending the chant which threatened to get out of hand.

They laughed as Martin opened the door for them. The children raced across to the car, still singing a song about animals that ate nuts. The father paused in the doorway.

"I won't forget about the bread," he promised.

As the little family drove away, Dannie added up the extra money.

"I think we need a treat," he said. "It's been grim. As soon as we've finished here, back to my place. We'll pick up a takeaway."

He saw Martin's glance, half hopeful, half afraid that he wasn't included.

"You and Blue too. Give your mother a chance to sit back and enjoy peace and quiet for once. My mother always said that was *her* greatest treat."

There was nothing that needed hand feeding. Fish for the seagulls, food for the owls, buckets of feed for the larger animals. Water for everyone and seed for the birds that weren't fish eaters.

There was more debris thrown around than usual. Martin, tidying up crisp and chocolate wrappers, wished people wouldn't throw their rubbish on the ground for others to pick up.

He checked all the pens. People sometimes threw their litter in there. Even a small piece of polythene could mean an expensive operation, or a death if not discovered in time, if one of the birds or animals swallowed it. And they would, if it smelled of food.

At last every bird and animal was fed, and locked in for the night. The foxes could never be kept out. They had already lost geese and two of their bantam cockerels. The fox that damaged Rosie was an early visitor who hadn't waited for night. Anna Wyn now shut her charges in before going home for tea, although it was still daylight.

Once the fox knew where to come, he would be back again.

Taid's dogs greeted them with wagging tails, and sniffed at the paper carriers which contained the food. Dannie warmed plates and boiled a kettle and Blue settled down with his two friends. All three watched hopefully, lest someone dropped a morsel on the floor.

Rosie's beak poked out of her little shed. Dannie went out to her, gave her her supper, and then closed the door.

"I get foxes too," he said.

Suddenly they were joking and talking, and having a party. Martin wondered when they had last laughed, and enjoyed themselves. It seemed a lifetime ago. He felt guilty, thinking of Taid. But the old man would be the last to condemn them to misery.

Darkness came unexpectedly. Time had passed so fast. It hid the fields and hid the mountains, though here and there they were patched with light from an isolated farm. Lights hung in the air, divorced from the buildings that held them. Lights sparkled along the streets and glittered round the coast.

Headlights scythed the sky, flashed and were gone.

"Life goes on," Dannie said, as they washed the dishes and put the plates away. "There has to be a solution. I don't believe in giving up."

"I don't know why you do so much for us," Anna Wyn said.

Dannie turned to look at her.

"Don't you?" he asked. "Just think about it. I have very good reasons."

Martin had never seen his stepsister blush before.

"I guess Blue could do with a walk," Dannie said. "I'll bring Anna Wyn home later."

Martin closed the door behind him and stroked his dog.

"Nobody but you ever wants me," he said. He looked up at the sky, and the new moon hanging in it.

"Wish on the new moon and your wish will be granted." Taid's voice whispered in his ear.

"I wish I had a real family," Martin breathed to the night, and knew as he said it that miracles never happened.

Behind him, in the cottage, he heard Dannie laugh.

It was very warm and sleep would be a long time coming. Martin walked on the hill, and looked down at the farm. Blue nudged his hand, reminding his master he was there.

There were lights in Taid's cottage and lights in Bryn Gwynt. His mother must feel almost as lonely as he did. He wondered why that thought had come to him. Gwyn had no time for any of them. He was walking in a fog of worry that had taken over his life.

Martin whistled to Blue who was nosing the ground, identifying the creatures that had walked that way. He began to run, enjoying the slight wind in his hair and the springy ground beneath his feet. He reached the kitchen. His mother turned and smiled at him. He ran to her and hugged her, surprising both of them.

Gwyn, coming in, glanced at Martin.

"I put something in your room for you," he said. "I wasn't prying."

Martin stared at his stepfather, wondering why Gwyn should feel he was unwelcome in any room in his own house.

"Thanks," he said, feeling awkward and unsure of himself.

Blue settled down in his corner of the kitchen and Martin went up to his bed. It was covered with newspaper, and laid out on it, in gleaming array, were all Taid's tools.

Martin stood for a long time at the window, too choked to go down and thank his stepfather.

Later, as he lay in bed, he knew he would ask Dannie to teach him how to carve animals and maybe between them they could go into business and help finance the farm. If only he could grow up now, and not have to wait so long.

The moon hung low in the sky. The wind cried in the trees, but even as Martin thought how quiet it was there was an appalling outcry. Every creature in the sanctuary was yelling, Skippy's demented brays drowning the rest of them.

Martin ran faster than he had ever done before, down the stairs and out into the strident and terrified night.

Chapter 16

"There's someone in the sanctuary!"

There were squeals and squawks and then an enraged hissing. Two boys and a girl charged towards the gate, all caution forgotten, with Tarr, the big gander, in fierce pursuit.

Tarr always protected his flock, and he was furious. His powerful body half flew, half walked. Neck outstretched, beak open, he was a terrifying sight. And he was winning the race.

The lads vaulted the gate and the girl climbed over. Slower, she had one leg safely across the top when Tarr hit, and bit her hard. She screamed, and fell on the wrong side.

Her friends were out of the yard, fast, leaving her behind. Dannie gave chase, but decided that he could probably find out their names from the girl, who was still shrieking, as Tarr readied himself for another attack.

Martin called to Blue, who ran through the now open gate and drove the enraged gander off his victim. She stood, tears streaming down her face.

"It's broken my leg. Hateful beast." They could barely understand her for sobbing. Anna Wyn was angry, but she couldn't leave the girl to go home as she was. "You couldn't stand if your leg was broken. Come on, into the kitchen." She had no sympathy at all and felt that the girl thoroughly deserved all she had got.

The intruder was muddy and bruised and obviously very shocked. Martin whistled to Blue, and walked over to Tarr, who had relaxed into his normal self now the danger was over.

Anna Wyn came back to the gate.

"She'll survive," she said.

Martin was so angry that he had to explode.

"I wish she'd broken her neck. I wish they'd all broken their stupid necks. What the hell's the matter with them? Why can't they leave us alone? I'd like to have a go at them, the lot of them. Useless stupid idiots. But at least I can tell *her* what I think of their antics."

"Hey, hey, calm down," Anna Wyn said. "What *were* they doing?"

"Opening every door they could. They've either wrenched off padlocks, or broken fences or cut through wire. Practically every bird and animal is out. They must have been here for an hour or more."

He banged his hand down on the top of the gate so hard that it hurt, which did not help his rage.

"At least we can get the names of the other two from that useless lump. It's a police case, and I hope they throw the book at them. I'd jail them for life. What good are they to anyone? I'd like to put an electric fence round the sanctuary; a powerful one that would give intruders one hell of a shock."

"Cool it," Dannie said wearily. "I'll ring the police. Then we've work to do."

Hours of work lay ahead. Heaven only knew if the animals had been injured, and some of them would certainly have been hurt while trying to escape from the mayhem. Why hadn't they heard anything?

It was easy to see why when they investigated. Wire had been cut, and anything that could be pulled out of the ground quietly had been pulled out. The wind, keening round the house, had drowned the first sounds that the animals made. Also the Sanctuary was some distance away from the main buildings and the nearest fields, and the wind was blowing in the wrong direction.

The broken cages needed repairing. Heaven alone knew what had happened to the little birds. Canaries, budgerigars, and both cockatiels had flown up into the trees.

Gwyn appeared in the yard as Anna Wyn went

back into the house. Dannie drove the tractor out of the barn, its lights flooding the sanctuary. He went back for the searchlights which ran off the tractor engine.

"Now what?" Gwyn demanded. "What's going on?"

"Someone's opened all the cages and huts and sheds," Martin said. The girl had come to the kitchen door.

"It's wicked to keep them caged like that," she said. "Making money from them. Using them for your own benefit. They don't have any life. I hate farmers. How dare you breed animals and then kill them for people to eat? It's disgusting. No one needs to eat meat."

"So that gives you the right to terrify every creature here? Animals that have learned to trust people, that no one has ever hurt in their lives. The little birds will be killed by the sparrowhawks and magpies and owls. Some of the animals will have injured themselves getting away from you . . . you . . . not us! We care for them, feed them, keep them safe and you come in like raving monsters full of daft theories and think you know it all. I hoep your leg is broken. I wish you'd broken your stupid neck. I wish the gander had killed all three of you."

Martin was too angry to care what he said. He advanced towards the girl, who stepped back hurriedly into the kitchen, staring at him in horror.

"Martin, there's work to do." His mother turned

145

to the girl. "Come inside and let's clean you up. You can have a cup of tea while we wait for the police."

The girl moved hurriedly, trying to get to the door, but Leah was too quick for her. "Oh, no you don't. There's payment to be made, my lady and you're making it. Anna Wyn, I'll take over here. I'll join you in the Sanctuary as soon as I can."

"I hope you don't find any of them. I hope they've all run away and are free, as God meant them to be," the girl shouted.

"And what sort of life do you think they'll have if we don't get them back into safety?" Gwyn demanded. "The foxes will have everything that lives on the ground, and the other animals will probably injure themselves. Half these creatures are lame or unable to fly, because they were badly injured. They can't look after themselves. You people make me sick. Why don't you think things through?"

The girl changed her tactics. Martin thought he knew her from school, where there was a small Animal Rights group among the sixth formers.

"Your goose nearly killed me. My father will sue you for keeping dangerous animals. Imagine that in a playground full of children. You have children here every day."

"He's safely penned," Anna Wyn said. "You let him out. Do you want that cup of tea or not?"

146

"I don't want anything to do with any of you. You all ought to be prosecuted by the RSPCA."

"And you, miss, and your two friends are going to be prosecuted for criminal damage," Gwyn said angrily. "Look at those pens and cages."

"We were doing the birds and animals a favour," the girl said.

Dannie, en route to the tool store, paused and stared at the girl.

"I know you, don't I? The dear little girl who sprayed foam all over the beagles when they were hunting. I hope you'll be pleased to know that one of them is now blind, thanks to you. They are animals too, with a right to be safe from criminal hooligans."

The police car drew up at the gate.

"Well, well," Dafydd Jones said, looking at the girl. "I might have known that if there were animals about you would be involved. Don't need to ask who the lads were. We can pick them up any time. Trouble, the whole lot of you."

"We were only thinking of the animals," the girl said. She stared at them, her face sullen.

Martin was already back in the sanctuary with Dannie, who was now armed with wood, rolls of wire, hammer and nails. Gwyn joined them a few minutes later. Caley, in his stable, which had not been noticed as it was at the back of the barn, was hammering with a hoof against the wood, frightened by the din.

The two little mares had run in panic down to the

marshy end of the field, where frequent flooding left the grass sparse and the ground unstable. Both were bogged down, struggling.

Dafydd the Police joined them a few minutes later. He took one look and removed his jacket. Gently, he coaxed each mare out of the mire, and on to hard ground, where they stood, shivering with fright.

Martin led them back to their enclosure, and brought extra hay. Anna Wyn took bundles of it to clean the mud from the ponies. No one seemed likely to go to bed that night.

"We'll need a fifty-hour day tomorrow," Gwyn said, looking at the mess.

The goats had had a field day. There wasn't a tub plant left uneaten. The Shetlands had cantered over the flowerbeds, destroying the displays which Taid had tended so lovingly. The gate of the pig pen lay on the ground, its hinges wrenched off.

Rabbits and Guinea pigs hopped around, frightened by their unaccustomed surroundings. One Guinea pig was dead, trampled by a frightened pony. There should have been seven geese, as well as Tarr, but there were only five. The two big geese were missing. The little grey Chinese geese huddled in fright, with no safe pen for the night. They were put in Blue's shed. The fox would be back without doubt to see what was available.

Dilys, on her return, found everyone still looking for birds and animals. Tony, the new young vet, who had driven her home, was soon part of the hunt.

By midnight most of the birds and animals were safely penned. Martin wished he could stay off school for good. They needed him here.

By two o'clock it was obvious that no more could be done. Some of the little birds had flown back to the familiar safety of their cages. Others were huddled, terrified by their strange surroundings, in the trees around the farm.

Dannie discovered one of the cockatiels in the tool store, and Leah almost fell over Sukie, the newest of the kids, who was cowering behind the big chair in the middle of the kitchen floor. The cause of all the trouble was driven home by Dafydd the police, who, Dafydd said ominously, would be calling on her and she hadn't heard the last of it by a long chalk.

Dilys and Tony bathed cuts and bandaged a broken wing. One of the pheasants had been kicked by Skippy, who was trembling in the stable next to Caley.

When Martin finally staggered to his bed, he fell asleep almost before his head hit the pillow.

Chapter 17

Four hours later, the ringing of Martin's alarm almost provoked him to throw the clock across the room. He dressed and went downstairs, snatching a buttered roll as he passed the kitchen table. Everyone else was already up, Gwyn working among his own animals, the rest of them in the sanctuary.

"We can't open," Anna Wyn said, almost in tears. "Look at the mess. We'll have to look under every shed and hutch, and search the trees. Even the chickens are missing."

"They're not all missing," Dannie said. They stared at him, triggered by the anger in his voice. "Come and look."

The fox had had a field day. Nine chickens and two cocks lay on the ground, their heads and feet

150

bitten off. Piles of feathers showed that the others had been plucked and eaten.

"We're back to where we started," Anna Wyn said, as she surveyed the chaos. "No flowers, no flower beds; it looks like a tip. There isn't a cage or hutch or shed that hasn't been damaged. They must have been here for hours."

"Watched till we went out," Dannie said. "Clever, but they'll have to pay. They haven't just released animals. There's a lot of damage here, and that's a crime, even if freeing birds and beasts to be killed by all kinds of hazards, is not. Or is it?"

Nobody knew.

Martin had never seen Dannie angered before.

"I hope Tarr really hurt that stupid little devil," he said. "I had immense trouble keeping my hands off her. Maybe she'll think twice about her friends in future. they left her to take the rap."

"She told us who they were." Anna Wyn was watching the second Shetland pony, who had behaved very oddly ever since her rescue from the marsh.

"Look at Dollie. She's had her foal. Where is it?"

The foal was still missing when Martin had to leave for school. He spent the day in a fog, angry and miserable, wishing that he were at home, helping clear up the mess.

As soon as he reached Bryn Gwynt, he rushed across the yard, whistling to Blue, and walked into the Sanctuary. Dannie and Mervyn were walking towards him, carrying a small animal. They laid it at Martin's feet.

Dollie's foal. It was beautiful, a tiny perfectly formed little creature, covered in mud which they had tried to wipe off. It was dead.

"Where was it?"

"She had it in the marsh. It drowned in mud. That little lot had better pay. I've a good mind to take it round to Mary's home and let her see what her meddling did. And take the dead chickens."

"Where's Anna Wyn?"

"At the vet, with an army of animals that hurt themselves one way or another. He'll have to come out anyway. Skippy must have jumped wire somewhere. He's gashed his underneath.

"All our winter feed money will go on vet bills," Martin said.

"The bills will be sent to the fathers of the three who came round here. Direct from the vet. Dafydd says they'll have to pay." Dannie slammed a nail in with satisfaction.

It was over a week before the place was tidy enough for visitors. The owners of a local nursery, hearing what had happened, came round with boxes of bedding plants. Mervyn and Dafydd both came in each day to help, so that Anna Wyn could be free to dress injuries and give medicine to her invalids.

Gwyn called his conference late on the Sunday night of that week.

"Taid was a remarkable man," he said. "I've

been going through his papers. It would have been easier if he had had some system, but everything was muddled up and he didn't leave a will. I knew he'd left me the farm by deed of gift, which meant that if he lived for seven years it would all be mine; if not, it would still be his, and we would have problems. I couldn't remember when he took that out."

They waited. Martin was afraid to breathe.

"Eight and a half years ago. So we are safe."

He looked round at the watching faces. Dannie had been asked to stay.

"Taid was still the technical owner. He made sure I paid for all the machinery. It used to rile me . . . I never realized that he had a very good reason."

Leah stared at him.

"I thought that you were arguing about your share of the farm," she said. "That there would be huge death duties . . . "

" Farms are different," Gwyn said. "I was arguing about his share of the new tractor. As he pointed out, he never used it, and he only gave a very little time to the farm, helping out where he could. I found it difficult at times to make ends meet as he never would pay any of the running costs. They all came out of my share of the profits, or our overdraft. We very rarely had any profit . . . more like losses last year."

"What happened to his money? "

Leah brought a plate of pasties and mugs of coffee, and handed them round.

"He left it in a family trust. I've only just found it, in a black box he kept at the back of his wardrobe, together with the deed of gift. He would never put them in the bank. I began to think he'd lost them or forgotten what they were and torn them up. He never told me about the trust. It's split between the girls, and last year he added Martin. Martin doesn't get his share until he's eighteen.

"There's income for Anna Wyn and Dilys now. Not a lot, but it might make the difference between life and death for the sanctuary. I don't know yet."

"We can make a go of it," Dannie said. "Martin and I are full of ideas which will bring in much better returns from visitors."

"We still can't pay you a wage." Gwyn said. "I don't know why you stay on here."

"Because I'm going to marry Anna Wyn. Not yet; in about eighteen months' time, we reckon. Which makes me family."

They stared at him. Anna Wyn's face was a sudden fiery red, but her eyes laughed as she looked at Dannie, who took her hand across the table.

"I hope there are no complaints," he said.

"We're delighted." Leah kissed them both, and looked at Gwyn who sat speechless. Then he grinned.

"I must say that she's chosen well. A nice strong man to become part of the family and help with the farm. And maybe later both Dannie and Martin can become partners."

"Unless Martin wants to be an accountant," Dannie said.

"I want to work on the sanctuary. Make it a business. Make it a going concern, so that whatever the EEC throw at us, we can survive." Martin was suddenly aware that he was being listened to, that his opinion counted, and that he had a major contribution to make.

He sat back, and then realized that within two years he would have money of his own.

"I'm leaving school at sixteen . . . " He looked at his mother, his eyes begging her to stifle her protest. "No. Listen to me. If there's enough when I'm eighteen I can go to veterinary college. Up to then I can study accountancy at night school. By the time I start college I'll have so much more animal experience, and when I've finished you won't need a vet . . . I'll be able to do everything necessary. Maybe have a surgery here too for local animals, though I'd rather farm."

"I'll give the sanctuary a year," Gwyn said. "At present the money made in the summer won't cover the winter. Anna Wyn doesn't want to spend all her money on animals in need of help. That has to change. Either we use the Animal Park to diversify in other ways as well, or we find something else that's much more profitable." He looked around the table at the watching faces. "All these lame ducks that come to you for food and medicine . . . they cost a fortune, and vet bills won't get cheaper. Nothing will. Martin won't be qualified for another seven years."

Seven years. It sounded like eternity.

"We ought to charge everyone who brings us a pet they don't want," Dannie said. "Nobody ever thinks of our running costs, only that Junior is bored with his rabbit or guinea pig, or that we can finance the hatchlings. Like that man who took eggs and hatched them and brought us the day old birds, thinking he was doing us a favour!"

A year for the sanctuary. In a year Martin would be nearly seventeen. He could work full time, and he knew that would make an immense difference. There would be time to think and plan and build.

"Can we have two years?" he asked. "So that I have a year to work out ways of making it better, after I've left school."

"I wanted you to stay on," his mother said. "You need A levels to get to college."

"A year at Tech will take care of those," Martin intended to work till he dropped if it would help. There were long vacations at college. He could spend them on the farm and he'd be learning all the time.

"There may be no future in farming," Gwyn said. "I appreciate that, Martin. You've a lifetime ahead and anything may happen. You need other skills."

156

"If I qualify as a vet I'll have another skill," Martin said. "I can get them at night classes. And I will. Can even do an Open University course. I'm never afraid of hard work, when I can see a point to it. I want to be here, want to be working with all of you; it's a family concern. If we have to give up the farm in years ahead, I'll still be a qualified vet. With my ideas and Dannie's . . . " His voice was alive with confidence.

Dannie laughed.

"Give us our heads," he said. "You don't know what you've got here. We're a good investment."

"Two years," Gwyn said. "Meanwhile we can celebrate."

"There's more to celebrate," Dilys held out her hand. A sapphire ring caught the light. "I'm going to marry Tony, so you'll have another vet in the family and a veterinary nurse. We can help here too. Maybe we can make it a double wedding. "

"Not sure I can afford it," Gwyn said.

"Two weddings on the same day. One set of guests. It's a bargain," Leah said, her voice high with excitement.

Suddenly they were all fizzing as if they had been drinking champagne, talking and laughing, making plans.

Blue barked, and everyone looked at him. There was a scratching sound at the door. Leah opened it and stared down as Taid's two dogs walked in, went to Dannie, nosed him and then both went to their corner, and lay down.

"I reckon the Animal Rights campaigners have just paid me a visit," Dannie said. He grinned. "They were locked in. If the silly fools could see what happened. The dogs've come right here to be enslaved again!"

Gwyn was staring at them as if looking at ghosts.

"I thought they were dead," he said.

"We couldn't," said Leah. "So Dannie took them. He has Rosie the goose too."

There was a thump on the door. This time Dilys opened it.

"Oh no he doesn't," she said as the big goose waddled into the kitchen, and snatched a scone from a plate. "Rosie's here too."

"I felt bad about Taid's dogs," Gwyn said. "More sense than me, haven't you?"

"We still haven't enough to pay for the winter feed and vet bills," Anna Wyn said. "I don't suppose—

"We have." Martin interrupted her, putting a cheque down on the table. "I sold all Lola's babies. And we had to write about something that happened in the holidays. I wrote about the animals that were hurt when that stupid lot came in."

"So?" said Dilys.

"They heard about it at the pub. They had a bingo session. Matt's dad runs the pub, and Matt brought a cheque to school today. They raised over five hundred pounds. I got three hundred for the

Sanctuary. Lola can go to the boar again, and be our top money-maker."

"Two years," Gwyn said. "It's up to you. By then Martin will be nearly eighteen, and if it doesn't work it's not too late for him to change his ideas. He may not want to spend five years qualifying as a vet; there are easier ways of getting a degree."

Martin whistled to Blue, who came to him and nudged him, looking into his pocket for a treat. They walked together into the yard and looked at the sky and thought how far he had come in the last three years, and how far he intended to go in the years to come.

He had wished on the new moon for a family and it was new moon time again.

The lights on the mountains winked at the stars above his head. The wind sang in the trees, and whispered around the animals' pens. Hooves rustled in the straw and an owl hooted and was answered from the Sanctuary, where Ollie spent his time half blind and unable to fly.

"Help me help them to make it pay," he said to the moon.

Gwyn, coming outside, put an arm across Martin's shoulders.

"Wish on the moon," Martin said.

"I often do," Gwyn said. "Long ago, I wished for a son . . . for man's talk."

"And now?"

Gwyn smiled.

"I think I'll just settle for wishing that all of us

get what we want," he said. "And hope that we want what we get!"

They stood side by side in the darkness, watching the lights on the mountain go out, one by one.

"Life is like a long road," Gwyn said. "You're at the beginning. It twists and turns and there are lots of corners and crossroads. We never know what lies ahead."

He turned to look at the farmhouse.

"I'm halfway along the road. Taid came to the end of his. If we do half as well as he did, I'll be a proud man when it comes to the end of my journey. I wish I'd told him," he added.

Martin, delighted to be a confidante, looked up at the clouds that were playing with the moon.

"I think he knew," he said.

Gwyn squeezed his shoulder, and went indoors. Martin stayed outside for a few more moments, savouring his words. That "we" had been an offer, and he intended to take it. There would be difficulties, but maybe he did, after all, have a family of his own. He was still a loner, an outsider, but he had the key to the door that would let him in.

It was up to him.